Sherlock Holmes and the Copycat Murders

Center Point
Large Print

Also by Barry Day and available from
Center Point Large Print:

*Sherlock Holmes and the
    Shakespeare Globe Murders
Sherlock Holmes and the
    Alice in Wonderland Murders*

SHERLOCK HOLMES
AND THE
COPYCAT MURDERS

BARRY DAY

CENTER POINT LARGE PRINT
THORNDIKE, MAINE

This Center Point Large Print edition
is published in the year 2017 by arrangement with
MysteriousPress.com/Open Road Integrated Media.

The text of this Large Print edition is unabridged.
In other aspects, this book may vary
from the original edition.
Printed in the United States of America
on permanent paper.
Set in 16-point Times New Roman type.

ISBN: 978-1-68324-437-0

Library of Congress Cataloging-in-Publication Data

Names: Day, Barry, author.
Title: Sherlock Holmes and the copycat murders / Barry Day.
Description: Center Point Large Print edition. | Thorndike, Maine :
    Center Point Large Print, 2017.
Identifiers: LCCN 2017014593 | ISBN 9781683244370
    (hardcover : alk. paper)
Subjects: LCSH: Holmes, Sherlock—Fiction. | Watson, John H. (Ficti-
tious character)—Fiction. | Private investigators—England—Fiction. |
Murder—Investigation—Fiction. | Large type books. | GSAFD: Mystery
fiction.
Classification: LCC PR6054.A928 S543 2017 | DDC 823/.914—dc23
LC record available at https://lccn.loc.gov/2017014593

This one is for
SONNY
The Hound of the Baskervilles

CHAPTER ONE

Indeed you could, Watson—indeed you could."

"Indeed I could *what?*"

It was not the first time Holmes had interrupted one of my reveries.

"Indeed you *could* show these young fellows a thing or two about fighting when things get worse in South Africa—as they inevitably will."

"But Holmes, you've read my mind precisely," I spluttered, "but how . . . ?" And then I stopped, realising that, once again, I had fallen into his favourite trap for me.

Sitting as usual in the chair opposite mine, Holmes threw back his head in that paroxysm of silent laughter that was peculiar to him and clapped his bony hands together once in satisfaction. When he is in this mood small things amuse him immoderately.

"As a piece of applied psychology it is really quite elementary, my dear fellow," he replied when he had recovered himself sufficiently. "I could hardly fail to notice that when you entered the room and sat down you immediately picked up this morning's *Chronicle*, which I had left folded at the story of that rather gruesome double murder in Wapping. The slight shudder that passed through your body was a perfectly understandable reaction under the circumstances, since the couple were bludgeoned to death with a candlestick.

"Your gaze then drifted to the candlestick on our own mantelpiece, an obvious association of thought. Once there—and with violence on your mind—your eyes moved to the adjacent frame which holds the medal you were awarded for your conduct at the Battle of Maiwand. At which point you winced and rubbed your war wound—something I've seen you do a hundred times or more. Then you became truly abstracted and, without realising it, sat up straighter in your chair. Your hand brushed your moustache and you distinctly pulled in your stomach.

"It seemed a fair assumption that your mind had moved on to the current conflict and the old warhorse in you was beginning to paw at the ground. Having heard your views on the youth of today on more than one occasion, it was—as I say—an elementary deduction to infer that you were even now putting yourself in their place."

"Holmes," I said ruefully, for I can never withhold my admiration for long, "you never cease to amaze me."

"Come, come, old fellow, you should be used to my parlour tricks by now. Once they are explained the process is no more complicated than winding in a ball of twine. Anyone can do it. Why, even you can do it. Now, let me see . . ."

And he steepled his long thin fingers in front of his face as he concentrated.

How often had I seen that expression? And how relieved I was when I did, for it meant that that engine of a mind was in gear and no longer idling, consuming him with frustration at being underemployed.

Too often lately I had had cause for concern as I would come upon him pacing our small living room like a caged tiger, unable to settle for long at one or other of his evil-smelling chemical experiments or even find distraction in his beloved Stradivarius. On occasions like these even his shelf of Day Books provided only temporary relief and a brief grunt of what might pass for satisfaction as he contemplated some reference to a previous problem, now safely solved. Even that could prove a mixed blessing, since it would often cause him to turn a sombre gaze in my direction, as though all this inertia were my fault.

"The world has grown dull, Watson, deadly dull. Where are the great cases? Where are the great *criminals* now that Moriarty is taking his sabbatical . . . ?"

"But Holmes," I would invariably interject, "logic says that Moriarty died after that Alice in Wonderland business . . ."

"Then logic—like the law—is an ass. Moriarty is no more dead than I am—which, at this precise

9

moment, is not saying a great deal. He is my *alter ego,* old fellow, my *doppelgänger*, and while he hibernates a part of me sleeps, too." We had had this conversation or one like it too many times in the past year to make it profitable for me to pursue it further.

At such moments I seemed to detect a feverish gleam at the back of his eyes and my old concerns would well up. He was no longer, in some indefinable way, the man I had known before the traumatic Reichenbach episode. He had always been driven but there were now times—like this one—when his internal fires seemed about to consume him and I feared for the fragile balance of his mental health. It was, after all, not too long ago that I had had to summon up such authority as I possessed as his medical man—as opposed to his friend—and force him to take a holiday of sorts. Even though it had proved to be what I believe is called a "busman's holiday" and involved a case that had almost cost us both our lives, he had returned from it with his batteries perversely recharged. Now, however, I seemed to sense he was returning to that critical state of nervous exhaustion that I knew and feared. For the past couple of days there had been moments when I had the distinct impression that he was in remission and that something of significance was beginning to absorb him once more but a moment later I was no longer sure.

So here we sat on this morning in early September 1900 in postures identical to those we had adopted so many times before that we might well have been figures in a Grecian frieze, as the sun warmed the yellow brick walls of the houses opposite and the sounds of the city drifted through the partly open windows like an inadvertent overture to some cacophonous modern piece.

Finally Holmes spoke. "I have it. What, my dear chap, do you make of *that?*" The doorbell had just pealed below. "Pray describe our visitor."

"Let me see," I tapped my pipe against my teeth for added gravitas. "Not a hesitant ring. Therefore, no trembling maiden undecided as to whether she should unburden herself of some dread family secret . . . Not an aggressive ring. Therefore, no angry squire from the shires demanding satisfaction for some imagined wrong. No, a confident ring suggestive of a strong male hand . . . someone who has every right to be here . . . a man in the commission of his duty . . ." I glanced at my fob watch. "Too late for the postman—we heard him earlier . . . too imperious for a telegram . . ." I pondered for a moment. "I would venture to suggest an officer of the law . . . not Inspector MacDonald—the parsimony of the Scot is in *his* ring. No, if I were a betting man . . ."

"Which you are," Holmes interrupted, rather unnecessarily, I thought.

"If I were a betting man . . ." I refused to have my *denouement* undermined—"I would plump for the good Inspector Lestrade."

The expression on Holmes's face was a veritable study—veiled surprise crossed with genuine amusement and, I thought I detected, a touch of genuine respect. It was a good moment, made even better when Mrs. Hudson knocked, put her head around the door and announced—"Inspector Lestrade to see you, Mr. Holmes."

I thought it superfluous to inform my friend that I had earlier intercepted a note from Lestrade indicating his intention to call at this hour. After all, we consulting detectives have certain trade secrets of our own.

Lestrade bustled into the room. The man has always struck me as having the air of a self-important whippet although, to be fair, he has more of the bulldog about him once he has been pointed at the right quarry. Holmes has always referred to him as the pick of a bad lot. Just as one finds oneself locked into a pattern of behaviour when faced with one's schoolmaster, an older relation or anyone who represented authority in one's early years, so Lestrade always seemed to me to display an amalgam of bravado and submissiveness in my friend's presence. Today was no exception.

"Morning, Mr. 'Olmes . . . Doctor." The battered bowler was being turned in nervous hands as he took the proffered chair and arranged his inevitable mackintosh around him with the care of a dowager at a society tea party. "Just happened to be in the neighbourhood and I thought . . ."

"You *thought?*" Holmes interrupted. "Excellent, Lestrade, excellent!"

Deciding that, once again, he was the butt of my friend's somewhat questionable humour, Lestrade laughed rather more than the pleasantry was worth and, having had his fun, Holmes—who had a genuinely soft spot for the man—now leaned forward in his chair.

"So pray tell us in what way my friend and I can be of assistance to you this fine morning?"

"Well, since you mention it, Mr. 'Olmes, there is one small thing you might be able to help us with." He rearranged the folds of his coat more precisely to avoid catching Holmes's eye.

"My lads were called early this morning to a house out Bayswater way. Landlady took the usual early morning tea and newspaper to one of her lodgers—a Mr. Montague. Second floor front. Knocked several times but couldn't make him hear. Finally got one of the other gentleman 'guests'—she calls them—to force the door. They go in and find Montague stiff as a bloomin' post sitting at the table. He'd been strangled. Well, I won't say that's all in a day's work for us at the Yard but we have seen a few in our time, haven't we?"

When Holmes showed no sign of responding, Lestrade continued.

"Well, I got over there sharpish like. I always tell my lads to move nothing. It's a little rule we professionals have. 'Who knows but what the smallest detail may contain the whole story?' I say to them . . . The rub on a man's cuff, a woman's glove, a stray hair . . .'"

I tried to catch my friend's eye without success but I could see that the corner of his mouth was trying not to twitch.

"An excellent *modus operandi*, Lestrade. Watson, perhaps you will be good enough to take a note?" Holmes had now tired of the badinage. "And what detail did you observe? Omit nothing, no matter how insignificant it may appear. It has always been one of *my* cardinal rules that the little things are infinitely the most important."

"Only this, Mr. 'Olmes, but I thought you should see it." And the Inspector extracted a folded piece of paper from an inside pocket and passed it across.

As Mr. Holmes unfolded it, I rose and went to stand behind his chair, so that I could read it over his shoulder. It was a sheet of ordinary cheap stationery and the words were made up of letters cut from newspapers. The variations in typography made it obvious that several different papers had been employed. It said—

JABEZ WILSON
REQUIESCAT IN PACE

"Jabez Wilson!" I exclaimed, "why isn't he the fellow who . . . ?"

"The victim of the so-called Red-Headed League and dead, poor fellow, these many years? The very same, Watson, the very same."

Handing the paper back to Lestrade—"I see entirely why you would wish to bring this to my attention, Inspector. If you have no objection, Doctor Watson and I will impose further on your good offices?"

"Certainly, Mr. 'Olmes, what did you have in mind?"

"Since the weather is fine, what do you say, Watson, to a little day trip to, say, Bayswater?"

CHAPTER TWO

The house was a three storey terraced affair in a quiet square just off the Bayswater Road. Looking back as we got down from the hansom that Lestrade had chosen over a more obvious police vehicle I could see Hyde Park. The prospect of people strolling idly in the late summer sunshine seemed a stark contrast to the sight I knew was waiting for us.

The open door was guarded by a uniformed policeman attempting to be as inconspicuous as a London bobby ever can. In the cramped, over-decorated hallway, positively reeking of gentility, a tearful middle-aged lady was being comforted by one of her lady "guests." I don't know quite why but I gained the distinct impression that her hysteria was tinged with more than a little excitement. The square was in for its share of gory details the moment Lestrade and his men packed up and left.

Lestrade himself was sufficiently impressed by the lady's performance, however, to remove his hat as he squeezed past her. Holmes and I, I regret to say, did not.

At the top of the narrow staircase a door stood open and a moment later the three of us—the constable having waited by the front door—were

16

standing in a small room which appeared to have suffered from the hand of the same decorator who had furnished the hall, almost certainly the landlady herself.

Overstuffed armchairs with antimacassars, potted plants in profusion, spindly tables covered with knick-knacks from foreign parts. Every surface it was possible to cover was covered with wallpaper or drapery and every cover seemed to boast a striking but strikingly different pattern. If not exactly a sight for sore eyes, it was a sight to make eyes sore.

And yet none of this prevented my eye being drawn immediately to the centrepiece of this gaudy stage set.

Sitting in an upright chair next to a writing table and slumped over it, as if, tired by his literary labours, he had just laid his head to rest on his folded arms for a quiet nap, was the figure of a man I judged to be in his late thirties or early forties. But the thing about him that shouted out to the heavens was . . .

"His hair, Holmes—look at his *hair!*"

The dead man had a full head of the most flaming red colour hair I had seen since . . .

"*Someone's,* I grant you, Watson, but most certainly not his."

And with a rapid movement of his gloved hand Holmes plucked off a red wig and held it up to the light. The suddenness of the gesture caused

Lestrade and myself to draw in our breath as one, while the dead man seemed to settle deeper in his chair, as if glad to be rid of the alien encumbrance.

"As I thought." Holmes had now turned the wig inside out and was peering at a label. "Nathan's theatrical costumiers. Suppliers to just about every stage production throughout the land. Though I very much doubt that our murderer will have been naïve enough to leave us a trail through their record of rentals. No, I fancy some unfortunate production will find their Property Department somewhat depleted. Watson, would you be good enough . . . ?"

I went over to examine the body. Rigor mortis had set in and I quickly determined that the man had been dead a good twelve hours or more. It would take a postmortem to be more specific. The cause of death, however, was quite clear. I turned to Holmes.

"The murderer stood behind him, leaned over and seized him by the throat. There are no signs of a struggle, which would seem to suggest that he was either taken completely by surprise or that he knew his assailant well enough not to be suspicious."

I held up the murdered man's right hand. "No defensive indications that he clawed his attacker's hands, no skin or blood under the finger nails. I would say he was taken totally by surprise."

I moved aside to let Holmes conduct his own examination. He concentrated on the marks around the neck, moving the head—sparsely coated with hair now that the wig had been removed—from side to side as he studied the indentations in the flesh made by the murderer's fingers. He muttered to himself, as I had heard him do so often. It was as if he were dictating notes to himself in an undertone. The face, as usual, might as well have been a mask, the features drawn, the brows set in two hard black lines.

While giving him room to work, I stayed close to the table and it was then that I noticed something odd. On the other side of the table but not close enough for the man to reach was an ash tray with the dottle from a pipe. What was odd was that, although it was clearly fresh— and the pin bright neatness of the room made it inconceivable that that landlady would leave it from one day to the next—the victim had no pipe. Nor did a quick survey of the room reveal any other signs of his having been a smoker.

Rather proud of myself, I related my findings to Holmes who was regarding the body thoughtfully, his finger to his lips. Without a single word of praise or even conjecture, he took the inevitable envelope from an inside pocket, moved to the other side of the table and tipped the ash into it. Only then did I receive a perfunctory, "Good work, Watson."

It was Lestrade who brought him out of his reverie.

"All right to move him now, Mr. 'Olmes?"

Suddenly it was as though a switch had been thrown and my friend returned to us from wherever he had been.

"Certainly, my dear Inspector, there is nothing more for us to learn here."

And with that he had swept from the room, leaving Lestrade and myself to follow in his wake. Thus it was Holmes who was the first to enter the hallway, where Mrs. Gentility—as I had begun to think of her—seemed somewhat recovered, thanks in part to the restorative powers of the purely medicinal brandy of which she and her lady guest were presently partaking.

As Holmes made to pass her with a slight tip of his hat, the lady of the house called out to him. "Oh, Mr. Holmes, you must be so upset at what's happened to your friend. He was one of the finest gentlemen as I've ever been pleased to have stay here."

Coming up close behind him, I saw Holmes freeze in his tracks. His head turned slowly to regard her properly for the first time. Behind me I heard Lestrade say—"You must be mistaken, Mrs.—er . . ."

"Cawston, Inspector—Mrs. Cawston. Oh, dear me no, there's no mistake. Mr. Holmes has been to see Mr. Montague half a dozen times these past few days. Why, I've let him in myself once or twice and Mr. Montague was always so pleased to see him. I don't know where I'll ever find another guest like him, I don't indeed . . ."

She was still continuing her monologue as we descended the steps and climbed back into the waiting cab.

I could see that Lestrade had a question on the tip of his tongue but the expression on Holmes's face seemed to persuade him that the moment was not the most timely. Making some excuse that he must stay and "check a few things with his lads," he instructed the driver and we were soon on our way back to Baker Street.

For the whole of the journey my friend said not a word and I knew better from the expression on his face than to try and coax one out of him.

The moment we were back in our rooms he did not even stop to take off his coat but hurried across to his chemical apparatus and busied himself with retorts, Bunsen burners and the ash he had scooped up in Montague's rooms.

As I hung up my own coat and hat I tried to recall all I could of the real Jabez Wilson. Readers of my little narratives of Holmes's early cases will perhaps remember the case of the Red-Headed League, in which Wilson, a pawnbroker, distinctive for nothing but the flaming colour of his hair, was duped into vacating his premises, while a gang of criminals used his basement to tunnel into the adjacent bank. The whole episode was over ten years ago and Holmes had solved it in his usual brilliant fashion, exposing the arch criminal, John Clay. Was this present business some strange form of long-delayed retribution? Surely not. In any case, I was almost sure I had heard Clay had died in prison. But then, what *was* behind this bizarre attempt to connect Holmes with the crime?

I could see that he had now brought his experiment to some form of conclusion and I attempted to lighten the strained atmosphere that pervaded the room.

"Well, old fellow, what have you determined? Something like this must be child's play to someone who has penned that definitive treatise, *Distinction Between the Ashes of Various Tobaccos*. Why, haven't I heard you say you can distinguish a hundred and forty different varieties of pipe, cigar and cigarette tobacco?"

Holmes looked at me for the first time since we had left the murder scene and there was the strangest expression in his eyes that I have ever seen. I would have said it was that of a hurt child peering out of that hawk-like face, if I hadn't immediately dismissed the thought as being ridiculous.

Then he spoke.

"Yes, it *is* child's play, Watson, but a rather disturbed child, I fear. I have identified the tobacco very readily. It is a coarse shag made up of an unusual blend of strands. There is only one mixture like it to my knowledge . . ."

"And that is . . . ?"

"My own."

CHAPTER THREE

In truth it was one of the strangest days I have ever spent in Holmes's company. I tried to imagine the sensations he must be experiencing. The analogy that kept occurring to me was that of someone turning a corner and bumping into himself. For a man so used to observing his fellow beings at a dispassionate distance, it must have been unnerving indeed to have that safe perspective torn away.

To begin with he seemed to put the conundrum to one side and made an effort—unusual in itself—to talk of other matters. The concert we were thinking of attending later in the week, the stultifying sameness of the items in the day's agony columns, those "rag-bags of singular happenings," as he always referred to them. Nonetheless, I knew my friend well enough to perceive that his mind was truly elsewhere and after a while the conversation began to peter out. He was relieved, I could tell, when I invented some urgent business that conveniently took me out of the house.

When I returned, having dined at the club, I found him sitting in an all-too-familiar posture. He was wearing his old mouse-coloured dressing gown and he had collected every available cushion in the room, denuding the sofa and both easy chairs in the process. He had piled them up into a sort of *ad hoc* divan in the middle of which he was sitting cross legged with an ounce of his favourite shag in front of him. He had settled on his stained old clay pipe and his gaze was fixed on the smoke from it as it wreathed around him and rose to form a cloud near the ceiling. It was Holmes at his most formidable.

The density told me that he had been there some time and, indeed, it was only intermittently that I could discern that Roman profile by the light of the one table lamp he had left burning. It was clear to me that this was more than a three pipe problem. An all-night sitting was in prospect and I knew better than to interrupt one of those. Wishing him a cordial, if subdued, "Goodnight," I closed the door and retired to my own room.

By the time I came down to breakfast the next morning there was no sign of Holmes. Mrs. Hudson had fortunately taken advantage of his absence to restore the room to some semblance of order. The cushions had been replaced and a window opened to clear the air of the tobacco fog. All would have been perfectly normal in our cosy little world, if it had not been for the nagging events of the previous day.

What could they possibly signify? Was Mrs. Gentility totally in error when she seemed to recognise Holmes? In my travels I have come across more than one lady of her kind, her eyesight requiring her to use spectacles but her vanity preventing it. Or was she, in fact, correct? Perhaps Holmes had some business with Montague that he was presently unable or unwilling to divulge and the man's murder had opened up some sinister by-way that was causing him his undoubted perturbation. Whatever the answer, I was sure of one thing. My friend's powers of deduction were infinitely more likely to resolve these questions than my own. As a result, I proceeded to apply them to the crossword in my morning paper, once I had done justice to Mrs. Hudson's ever-reliable breakfast.

The morning passed agreeably, as lazy mornings are apt to do and it was close on noon before the sun shining through the window tempted me to take a stroll, a stroll which wound up inevitably at my club. There, over a decent Beaune, I was able to settle most convincingly— at least to my satisfaction—an argument that had been left unresolved the previous evening. It really is most remarkable how one finds the *mot* or even the phrase *juste* the very moment after one leaves the scene of the crime, so to speak. Undoubtedly something to do with brain waves and word association. I resolved to bring it up with Holmes at some future and more propitious moment.

My thoughts were once again on him as I opened the front door of 221B. Mrs. Hudson was not there to answer my ring and I remembered it was her afternoon to visit her married sister in Clapham. As I climbed the stairs I could hear Holmes moving around in our rooms above and for some reason I felt a surge of relief at the accustomed sounds.

I positively burst into the sitting room and was chatting away nineteen to the dozen before I had even hung up my overcoat properly, regaling him with the way I had triumphed in my footling argument at the club. Even to my ears it sounded a little inconsequential and I was not unduly surprised that it did not exactly elicit an enthusiastic response from my friend.

In fact, now that I came to look at him, his manner seemed rather aloof but I put it down to the continued after effects of the previous day's unsettling experience. He had taken up his position by the window, where the afternoon sun turned him into a virtual silhouette.

Realising that my chatter was falling on near deaf ears and prompting only the merest of monosyllables by way of reply, I resorted to a device that never failed to soothe him when he was in an enervated state.

"Fancy a soothing pipe, old fellow? I don't know about you but it's been one of those days as far as I'm concerned."

And suiting action to utterance, I took a tin of my favourite Arcadia from the occasional table near my chair—as near to a shrine as I ever hope to get—pulled my trusty briar from my pocket and proceeded to fill it.

"Aren't you going to join me, Holmes?"

"Ah, yes, of course, Watson," he replied and moved hesitantly across to the fireplace, as if he were in two minds about even so simple a decision. Once there, he did the strangest thing. His hand began to grope around over the surface and I realised that he was looking for his pipe.

Before I could stop myself I had blurted out. "Now when was the last time you left any of your pipes there, old chap? You know what a fuss Mrs. Hudson makes about the marks. In the coal scuttle—where they always are . . ."

"Of course, stupid of me. Been a little pre-occupied today." And he busied himself ferreting in the aforesaid coal scuttle until he had pulled out a pipe that I could barely remember his using in ages. Then the vague look returned—until I quickly added: "Toe of the Persian slipper . . . if it's that terrible old shag of yours you're looking for. An appropriate and ingenious hiding place, I've always thought."

And then I laughed immoderately to hide what was becoming a very real concern for my friend's state of mind. I had seen him in all manner of moods over the years we had been companions and while this was not the hyperactive condition that resulted from the cursed needle, it was somehow even more worrying, since—to my knowledge—there was no medical condition to account for it.

Something of my own state of mind must have communicated itself to Holmes, for he immediately put down pipe and tobacco without even pretending to combine the two and hurried back to take his place by the window, his back half turned in my direction.

"Sorry, Watson. You must forgive me. Not myself today."

And with a last glance down into the street below, he positively dashed to the coat rack and began scrambling into an overcoat.

"I say, Holmes, are you sure you're all right? That's *my* coat you're about to make off with."

With a muttered apology he seized his own ulster and, without even bothering to put it on, was out of the door. I heard his feet clattering down the stairs, nearly coming a cropper on the loose carpet tread four from the bottom and then the front door slammed behind him.

I resumed my seat and puffed away trying to steady my own nerves and sort out my feelings about this bizarre little episode. Catching sight of myself in the large mirror over the fireplace, I observed grimly and without satisfaction the furrowed brow and realised that the roles had—for the moment at least—been ironically reversed. *I* was now the one with the three pipe problem. Though if *one* pipe couldn't solve it, nothing would.

What was I to do? As his friend and medical adviser I had twin obligations. Was this the mental breakdown I had so long feared for Holmes? Who could I talk to without breaking my old friend's confidence and setting off all manner of harmful rumours that might jeopardise who knew what delicate affairs?

Suddenly an idea came to me. Perhaps there was something in this tobacco-inspired therapy after all! An item I had seen in this morning's *Chronicle* came back to me and I snatched up the pages lying near my feet and began to riffle through them.

Ah, yes, there it was, a couple of unobtrusive paragraphs on an inside page that had only caught my eye because of a previous encounter . . .

CONTROVERSIAL MEDICAL MAN VISITS LONDON

Dr. Sigmund Freud Arrives to Address Conference

I could see that small bearded figure now sitting opposite Holmes and myself in the lounge at Brown's Hotel and hear that piping voice as it mangled the Queen's English. I had first viewed him, I must honestly confess, as something of a joke but—setting his appearance aside—what he had said to us that day had been instrumental in bringing to a safe conclusion one of the most complex cases my friend and I had ever encountered. I seem to remember the outcome had not displeased a certain lady in high places. But my thoughts were wandering off the point . . .

I noticed from the accompanying text that the good doctor from Vienna would be in town for another two days, staying once again at Brown's and resolved to renew our previous acquaintance without delay.

Still pondering on how I might best approach the subject when we met, I set about restoring the newspaper to some semblance of order. I do believe Holmes's aggravating habit of turning the morning press into a veritable ocean of crumpled paper has turned me into a fussier person than nature originally intended. While I was about it, I might as well save some of his wreckage.

Crossing over to his chair, I noticed to my surprise that his own collection of what I might call the more "popular" papers—chosen largely for the more melodramatic aspects of their crime and agony columns—had not even been disturbed but lay neatly folded as Mrs. Hudson delivered them every morning.

Instead, my arrival had clearly interrupted

31

Holmes in the perusal of one of his commonplace Day Books. For as long as I could remember he had been clipping and filing paragraphs that caught his eye concerning people and events. The most *outré* references were never more than a fingertip away. In this matter he was normally meticulous, taking care to replace the books as soon as he had finished consulting them in his own complex filing system that only he could comprehend. Nonetheless, he could lay his hand on any given reference within seconds. It was, therefore, most unusual, whatever the distraction, for him to leave one of his "Bibles" unshelved.

I picked up the volume in question and examined it. It was a new one that I hadn't seen before and seemed to be devoted entirely to Germany and German-related affairs. There were cuttings about the Hohenzollern dynasty and copious notes on Kaiser Willhelm II. Several articles dealt with the Socialist movement and outbreaks of civil insurrection in various states.

All of which was rather puzzling to me. Although I knew Holmes had an encyclo-paedaic mind, to my knowledge he had never demonstrated any particular interest in our cousins across the North Sea. I would have been prepared to bet, in fact, that he was instinctively impatient with what he regarded as their stolidity of mind. Come to think of it, the only positive remarks I had ever heard him make on matters

German had been in praise of the music of Wagner.

I returned to the page at which the book had originally been open when I had interrupted Holmes. It contained a series of clippings, some of them from German newspapers, pertaining to someone called Klaus Geier. From Holmes's annotations it appeared that he had been a minor diplomat who had surprisingly given up that staid vocation to become an actor. The laconic comment in Holmes's spidery scrawl employed yet another language—"*Plus ça change, plus c'est la même chose*!!" My eye was drawn to another of his notations. Next to an English language profile of Geier's stage career which included the phrase—"Geier is particularly proud of the fact that his name means 'eagle' in native language . . ." Holmes had scribbled "Pride goes before a fall. In fact, the word me 'vulture'! Ha!"

The printed text continued—"Key to recent success on various European stag Geier's consummate—some say unrival ability to . . ." Before I could read any m heard the front door open and Mrs. Hu voice saying: "Oh, Mr. Holmes, you mu second sight. I've only just this min back myself. I hope you've had a su day yourself?" Knowing how posse was about his files, I quickly replaced

33

in the gap on the shelf and resumed my seat.

As a result I didn't catch Holmes's reply before he had bounded up the stairs—in marked contrast to the way he had left—and was in the room.

"Ah, Watson, just the man I want to see. A quiet pipe and then a little something at Simpson's, I think. How would that suit you, old fellow? I'm sorry if I've been out of sorts lately but . . ."

His eyes read the expression in my face in a flash. I have never been good at dissembling at the best of times and I'm sure my features on this occasion were an open book to one who knew me so well. So marked was the contrast between the dour nervous Holmes of a few minutes earlier and the ebullient fellow who stood before me that I had trouble seeing the same man. All of this might as well have been blazoned on my brow.

Before I could find words to express any of it, I was literally saved by the bell. This time it was the frantic pealing of the front door bell, accompanied by Mrs. Hudson's muttered exhortations to the caller to hold his horses.

As one Holmes and I cried out—"Lestrade!"—and burst into laughter. It was the first time the tension between us had relaxed.

Then the sitting room door opened and a flustered Mrs. Hudson announced our visitor—the much anticipated and even more flustered Lestrade. Without even bothering with the usual courtesies, he thrust a note into Holmes's hand.

"There's been another one," he cried.

Once again I found myself reading over my friend's shoulder. There was the same kind of cheap notepaper, the same crudely cut and pasted letters. This time the message ran—

GRIMESBY ROYLOTT
REQUIESCAT IN PACE

CHAPTER FOUR

But Grimesby Roylott . . ."

"Precisely, Watson. *Requiescat*, certainly—since 1883, if memory serves. *In pace*, I very much doubt . . ."

We were bowling along once again in a hansom, courtesy of Lestrade, this time along the Embankment. The Inspector had insisted on a diversion via Scotland Yard to collect a Home Office pathologist en route. I suppose I could have taken it as a slight on my medical competence but that was the least of my concerns. Now we had *two* of these cryptic messages referring to two of Holmes's previous cases. What could it all mean?

In my mind's eye I could still see the distraught figure of Helen Stoner, sitting tense in her chair at Baker Street on that April morning as she shared with us her fear of her stepfather and of Roylott's brooding presence at Stoke Moran, the ancestral family seat where we had faced evil incarnate. Despite all that has happened since, I am still inclined to believe that it was the case which presented more singular features than any other in our long partnership. The very memory of it made me shudder involuntarily, despite the warm day and I reflected—not for the first time—on the way a smiling sun and a clear sky can be a deceptive mask for the sinister thoughts that lurk in the human heart.

Lestrade was clearly going through some equally contorted mental processes of his own as he sat opposite us turning the latest note this way and that, as if he expected it to suddenly reveal its secret, once he had it in the correct position. Finally, he gave up.

"Well, what do *you* make of it, Mr. 'Olmes?"

"I have made it a life rule, Lestrade, not to make bricks without straw or to theorise without adequate data. However, I am prepared to make one firm prediction . . ."

"And that is . . . ?"

"Whatever evidence that note may have been able to provide has certainly been obliterated by the way you have just been handling it. I have reason to believe, for instance, that the classification of finger prints, so ingeniously devised by Sir Francis Galton, is likely to be officially adopted by your lords and masters within a twelvemonth. After which, if there is any justice—which I am sometimes inclined to doubt—your recent behaviour would probably rank as a capital crime."

Then, seeing the flustered way the Inspector stuffed the note back into his pocket, Holmes relented, leaning across to tap his old sparring partner on the knee.

"Don't worry, Lestrade. If I had not satisfied myself that the writer had worn gloves and therefore left no identifiable marks on the paper, I should hardly have allowed you to continue. No, I think we shall find our friend, whoever he is, has made some small study of our methods and acted accordingly. Don't you agree, old fellow?"

"Indubitably," I replied for Lestrade's benefit. And then, as an aside to Holmes, I murmured— "It's certainly good to see you in better spirits than you were earlier this afternoon. A Holmes who can't even find his favourite pipe is a Holmes who is seriously out of sorts. I have often heard you refer to your pipe as a counsellor."

And I laughed—perhaps more loudly than the pleasantry deserved—until I found I was laughing alone. For Holmes was looking at me as though I had struck him.

"But I was not *in* Baker Street earlier this afternoon. My business took me to Dorking. And my favourite pipe is right here—in my pocket."

"Well, gentlemen, here we are," said Lestrade, once more stating the obvious, as the cab drew up outside a modern block of flats.

"The Speckled Band." Holmes was speaking more to himself than Lestrade or myself. Then, remembering our presence, he continued—"The somewhat melodramatic title you gave to your subsequent account of the case, Watson. There is little doubt that this was the cause of death . . ."

And here he held aloft a ladies' silk scarf, dark yellow in colour and patterned with large brown dots. Although it was but a poor literal replica of the deadly Indian swamp adder that had wrapped itself around its victims' heads before administering its fatal kiss, the symbolism was all too clear. Dr. Grimesby Roylott had employed one of those loathsome exotic creatures to work his grisly business on the Stoner sisters until Holmes had turned it upon its master.

The expression on the face of the dead man at the table bore all too close a likeness to the one we had witnessed on Roylott's that horrific morning in Surrey. The discoloured face with its protruding tongue, the eyes glazed and fixed on the ceiling in an eternal stare. There was only one significant difference and at that very moment Lestrade put it into words.

"Looks like he was strangled with that there scarf first and *then* it was tied round his head like some sort of Indian turban."

"Precisely so, my dear Inspector, I concur entirely. And presumably you noticed the way the scarf was knotted?"

"Oh—er—naturally, I noticed that immediately."

"Neatly tied with the end tucked in. Not the easiest thing in the world to dress someone else, particularly when death prevents them from being co-operative."

As he spoke Holmes was restlessly pacing around the room, his piercing eyes taking in the details of its furnishing. Unlike the fussiness of the Bayswater flat, this was a modern building and the furnishings clean and modern. As we had entered the building a few minutes earlier we had been greeted by the now familiar sight of the constable guarding the entrance as unobtrusively as possible. I was for some inexplicable reason relieved to see that it was not the same officer as the one we had encountered on the previous occasion.

We had been escorted to the fourth floor where another uniformed officer was keeping inquisitive neighbours at bay. In a small brass holder on the front door a card announced that the tenants in residence were a Mr. & Mrs. Simon Pettigrew— or rather, that they *had* been, since it was the late Mr. Pettigrew who was presently occupying my friend's attention. Mrs. Pettigrew—whose hysterical screams had raised the alarm on her return from an overnight stay with relations— was in the adjacent bedroom receiving tea and sympathy at the hands of her maid. I reflected on the pivotal role played by "a nice cup of tea" at times of crisis in English society. Perhaps Holmes could be prevailed upon to pen a short monograph on the subject when things got back to normal—whatever "normal" could now be con-sidered to be.

"Montague & Pettigrew. Montague & Pettigrew." Holmes was muttering as he continued his scrutiny of the room. "Sounds like a firm of lawyers in Dickens." It was a habit that often took him over at such moments of intense concentration, almost as if he were conversing with himself. Finally he stood back and turned in my direction.

"Well, Watson, you know my methods. What do *you* make of this little piece of theatre?"

"I'd say the fellow was taken by surprise, very much like Montague. No obvious signs of a struggle, so presumably his assailant came up behind him without causing suspicion . . ."

"Yes, yes, of course," Holmes interrupted testily, "but what else do you observe?"

"Ah," I rushed in with an observation I had been dying to make from the moment we had first seen the room. "The table is completely empty except for a small saucer of milk and a riding crop with a noose tied into the end of the lash. From which I deduce . . ."

". . . that someone is trying to replicate the circumstances of our earlier case. But since there *is* no serpent—although I must admit that this substitute . . ." (And here he flicked the scarf rather callously, I thought) ". . . has proved lethal enough, in all conscience—I think we may safely

41

consign them, too, to the department of theatrical properties, chosen with an eye to visual effect.

"No," he continued, his eye fixed on the far corner of the sparse little room, "I am more interested in your conclusions concerning the singular matter of the ash tray . . ."

"But there *is* no ash tray," I replied, looking hastily around the room to confirm my impression.

"*That* is the singular matter," my friend replied, "considering the man happens to be holding a pipe." And on that cue he hoisted Pettigrew back in his chair, so that the left hand, which had been hidden by the slumped position of the body, suddenly thumped down on the table top. Sure enough, clutched in the dead man's hand and almost engulfed by it was a pipe.

"Now then, gentlemen," Holmes continued, now including us both in his little dissertation, "when did you ever know a pipe smoker who did not have an ash tray ever at his elbow?"

The irreverent thought crossed my mind that I could think of at least one who thought nothing of tapping out dottle and debris wherever the fancy took him but it seemed an inappropriate moment to bring up domestic issues.

"Not only no ash tray but no matches, no tobacco pouch—in short, no means of *smoking* the pipe he clutches so tightly."

As he spoke, Holmes was doing his best to free

the object of his attention from the dead man's grasp but, although the murder was of fairly recent origin—as I had determined earlier on entering the room—*rigor mortis* had already set in and it took much of his considerable strength to wrest it free.

"Even more singular, gentlemen. Why should a man who is clearly right handed, as is evidence by the callouses and ink stains on his right fore-finger and who—by the same evidence—is not in the habit of exposing himself to the consumption of tobacco of any sort be holding an empty pipe in his *left* hand?"

"And if I am not mistaken, Watson,"—and here he turned to face me directly, holding up the pipe for my inspection—"this meerschaum is the pipe you seemed to think I was searching for earlier. Thanks to your accounts of our little adventures and the—shall we say?—'atmospheric' drawings of Mr. Sidney Paget with which *The Strand Magazine* chooses to embellish them, the general public is under the impression that such a pipe is inseparable from my lip. Whereas *you* know— and even you, Lestrade, may have had occasion to notice—that my pipe of choice is, in fact, *this* one . . ." And here he drew a stained old briar from his pocket. For an endless moment the two pieces of evidence were proffered side by side for our inspection.

And then someone else spoke . . .

"Oh, Mr. Holmes, who could have done this terrible thing?"

A frail middle-aged lady was standing in the doorway with an older woman in maid's uniform standing just behind her in anxious attendance. Under normal circumstances she must have had a faded prettiness but now she looked understandably strained and it was obvious that she had been crying for some time.

I looked at Holmes but his face was a mask.

Then, as if realising that the social niceties must be observed even at a time like this, she looked across at Lestrade and myself and motioned us to resume our seats, for rising had been an involuntary reaction on our parts—"Oh, forgive me, gentlemen, I am Mrs. Simon Pettigrew, the wife of . . ."

At which point she must have caught a glimpse of the body, even though Holmes had had the presence of mind to try and shield it from her with his own. She gave a little gasp and would have fallen, if the maid had not been close to support her. Making a supreme effort to control herself and with eyes carefully averted, she continued—"Catch them, Mr. Holmes—whoever took my Tom from me, catch them, I beg you. He hadn't known you long but he was inspired by your visits. 'There's a man who appreciates my work, Marge,' he'd say. The last words he said to me before I went away were—'This old country hasn't much to fear with Sherlock Holmes on her side, old girl.' "

And she broke out in a fresh paroxysm of sobs as she was led gently from the room with Lestrade and I bobbing up again in unison like a couple of rubber nine pins. Our expressions, too, were carbon copies of each other in their puzzled blankness.

Only Holmes seemed unshaken by what we had just heard. But then, was his apparent lack of reaction more or less concerning than our own? In another man I would have been outraged by what he said next.

"Montague, Pettigrew and . . . *who,* I wonder? In Dickens surely they were always in threes, weren't they? Except, of course, the Cheeryble Brothers. No, no, the cadence is certainly not complete."

Then, putting a pipe in each pocket of his ulster, he proceeded to tip his hat to the two of us. "I have a few personal matters to attend to, Watson. And I must not keep Mr. Dopple waiting. I may be some time."

Before either of us could think of a solitary word to say, he was gone. Downstairs we heard the constable murmur a few words of greeting and then the door was quietly closed.

It was Lestrade who spoke first but he was only putting into words something that was hovering like an ominous cloud in both our minds.

"Lumme, Doctor, am I hearing what I *think* I'm hearing? I mean, *one* of these ladies could have been mistaken—but *two?* It's not as if Mr. 'Olmes was exactly your run of the mill sort of bloke, now is it? And then there's all these bits and pieces of his at the scene of the crimes. You don't think . . . ?"

"No Lestrade, I do *not* think anything of the sort," I replied with more asperity than I truly felt in my present state of mind. In fact, if truth be told, I was using my anger with the totally blameless Inspector to help me control my own emotions.

"And who's this Mr. Dipple? Dapple?" he went on.

"*Dopple*. And I haven't the faintest idea." I hoped by my abrupt tone to stop him but he was a veritable fount of questions now.

"But, Doctor, who could have known the details of these old cases of yours?"

"Absolutely no one, Lestrade—except, of course, the several hundred readers who bought *The Strand Magazine* and the several thousand others who read it in their dentist's waiting room. That should give you a possible list of suspects to start with," I added with what I hoped was heavy irony.

Despite my bravado, I knew I had deflected his point without in any way answering it. If only

46

Holmes were here to . . . And then I realised the futility of this train of thought. As often happens at times of stress a completely lateral thought popped into my mind. It was a question that had puzzled my admittedly never very nimble brain in a logic exam many more years ago than I cared to remember.

"If an invisible man were sitting in that chair, that chair would be empty. But that chair *is* empty. Therefore an invisible man is sitting in it. Discuss." How could even Holmes solve a problem when he himself was at the very heart of it?

In my mind I went back over the events of the last few days and tried to think as my friend would—always supposing my friend still *was* my friend. The effort would at least help keep it from flying off in all directions. Now what would Holmes ask me?

What had I *seen* and what had I *observed?*

I could swear I had seen Holmes look as surprised as I was when the first note arrived and even fearful when he had analysed the tobacco ash and found it to be his own.

I had subsequently seen him sink into a mood of deep introspection—but, then, there was nothing remarkable in that. Quite out of character, though, was the disorientation of earlier in the day. It was as though he had literally lost his bearings—yet an hour or so later he was back to being the same Holmes I knew so well.

The *second* murder, now. There was something distinctly different about his behaviour there. It was almost as though he knew what he was going to find. Was this the demeanour of a trained mind investigating—itself? No, the idea was absurd and yet . . . And yet the meerschaum *was* the pipe he had picked up himself and he had made no attempt to pretend otherwise. "Pipes"—I could hear his voice speaking the words—"pipes are occasionally of extraordinary interest, old fellow. Nothing has more individuality, save perhaps watches and bootlaces."

And nagging at the back of my mind was another though that had occurred to me more than once when watching him at work. Had that focused energy and that remarkable brain been otherwise employed, he would have made the most formidable criminal who ever lived. We had joked about it more than once.

Had I actually seen him cross that divide to his own dark side?

And how could I possibly live with that fact— should it prove to *be* a fact?

CHAPTER FIVE

It was in this despairing mood that I returned to Baker Street, leaving Lestrade and his men picking over the Pettigrews' rooms in a desultory fashion. For once I sympathised entirely with the official forces of the law. What incentive was there when you were virtually certain you knew who to apprehend but couldn't bring yourself to accept what was staring you in the face?

But this was, it had to be faced, not a situation that could be of long standing. Any time soon—unless there was some dramatic turn of events—the wheels would begin to turn and I knew all too well that those wheels could grind exceedingly small. And even though Holmes—like Othello—had most certainly "done the State some service," in the nature of things he would be held accountable. But it would not—*could* not come to that. There must be some explanation I was missing—but what?

I was so abstracted as I let myself into our sitting room that at first I did not notice that I was not alone. Then a discreet cough announced someone's presence.

"Holmes!" I cried, thinking that he had returned to explain where my observations had led me astray and to put all right, as he had done so often.

"Holmes, indeed, Doctor. But not, I fear, the Holmes we were both hoping to find."

Spinning on my heel, I was aware of the massive bulk of Mycroft, Sherlock's elder brother, levering itself out of the depths of his sibling's chair.

It would be hard to imagine two brothers who resembled one another so little. While Holmes was lean and wiry with a tense expression never far away from his features, Mycroft was positively corpulent and his face totally impassive at all times. I could quite see why his colleagues in Whitehall referred to him as a "mandarin," for there was certainly an air of oriental inscrutability about him, as befitted someone who was privy to just about all of our nation's secrets. Although he carried no official title, he was—as Holmes had once confided to me—"the central exchange, the clearing house" of the British Government and in a world of specialists *his* speciality was omniscience. "Occasionally," he had added with a distinct touch of fraternal pride, "he *is* the British Government."

"My dear Mycroft," I said, when I had caught my breath, "other than our mutual friend there is no man in London I would rather set eyes on at this moment. You can have no concept of the events of the past two days. Why . . ."

". . . and Phipps," Mycroft replied before I could say anything more.

"I beg your pardon?"

"Montague, Pettigrew and *Phipps*. A name that, I must admit, sounds uncommonly like a questionable law firm in a minor Dickens novel . . ."

Was extra-sensory perception built into the Holmes family genes, I wondered?

". . . unfortunately the significance of these three gentlemen does not lie in the realms of fiction. Had it done so, I should hardly have embarked upon this pilgrimage half way across London."

I reflected that "half way across London" consisted of the relatively short cab ride from Mycroft's Pall Mall club but then he had long since chosen to circumscribe his physical existence by restricting his universe to the club, his lodgings immediately opposite and Whitehall. When he made one of his rare visits to Baker Street—and I could think of only four previous occasions—it was, as Holmes put it, akin to a planet leaving its orbit.

One thing was sure. There would be a most potent reason for this diversion.

"But, Doctor . . ."—Mycroft's voice brought me back from my reverie—"I fear I am disturbing the even tenor of your ways. Pray remove your overcoat and make yourself . . ." And he had the grace to pause as he realised what he was about to say.

I shrugged off my coat and went to hang it up on the coat stand in the corner of the room but I must have been more shaken than I knew, for somehow I clumsily managed to knock the whole contraption over, spilling hats, coats, umbrellas and walking sticks on the floor. Refusing Mycroft's offer of help with perhaps insufficient courtesy, for I was annoyed with myself, I replaced everything as near as I could recall in its original place. For myself I should have taken less trouble but Holmes was a stickler for everything being in its appointed place, even if he did work to some impenetrable code of what should go where that I have never been able to fathom.

The last item was one of his own coats. It had fallen awkwardly and as I scooped it up, something fell out of one of the pockets. A series of small dried objects that I picked up and lay on the palm of my hand.

Suddenly I felt a sensation like that of someone running an icicle down my back. What I was holding was a handful of—dried orange pips!

And now Mycroft's voice was close to my ear as I knelt there.

"I think the most appropriate word might be— 'SNAP!' "

A beefy hand appeared next to mine. The

fingers unclenched and there on the palm were five identical orange pips.

"And I very much fear that is not the end of the coincidence, Doctor." As we rose he presented me with that by now familiar note. This one read—

JOHN OPENSHAW
REQUIESCAT IN PACE

"The man Holmes sent to his death in the Case of the Five Orange Pips?" I heard myself say as I sank into my chair.

"The very same." Mycroft was pacing the room now, if the ponderous motions of a man-o'-war can be described as pacing.

"Although I have always believed—as I know you have, Doctor—that my brother scourged himself unduly on that issue, there was no way he could have known the man was in such mortal danger. Technically, however, you are correct. John Openshaw or—as he was known in the real world—William Phipps—was the third of the men killed in a manner that echoed a specific crime investigated by my brother, the well-known consulting detective, Sherlock Holmes.

"Phipps was strangled just over an hour ago in his bachelor rooms in Albany. The orange pips were found on his distended tongue. Only the fact that the Head Porter is personally known to me and well aware of my interest in Phipps and any possible visitors ensured that I was informed ahead of the police. A few discreet enquiries enabled me to ascertain that you and the indefatigable Inspector Lestrade were engaged on what might be described as parallel business. I considered it a reasonable assumption that you would return here directly and that you would be alone. I see that I was correct on both counts. Mrs. Hudson considered me sufficiently trustworthy to permit me to wait and . . ." He gestured expansively around the room that suddenly seemed smaller for his presence.

And then—for no reason that made logical sense—I felt as though a great weight had been lifted from my shoulders. Here was the one man to whom I could unburden myself without being disloyal to Holmes. After all, had it not been Mycroft he had chosen to keep his secret when the world thought him killed at the Reichenbach Falls? I still felt the odd twinge of jealousy when I thought of that episode but it was a very long time ago and blood *should* be thicker than the water of friendship.

Before I knew it I was pouring out my concerns and theories about these copycat killings. In spite of the anxiety of the moment, the storyteller in me could not help planning how he would eventually tell the tale—providing there was to be a tale that would stand the telling.

When I had run out of both breath and suppositions, Mycroft hoisted himself out of Holmes's chair once more.

"Doctor, I believe what we both need right now is a sustaining little something at my club. As I think you know, the food is reasonably palatable, the wine perfectly acceptable and the privacy unparalleled. And over our repast I have a tale to tell you which will either illuminate recent events or throw them into even deeper gloom. If you are ready, the planet may perhaps resume its orbit." And he gave the vestige of a smile. "Shall we . . . ?"

An hour later—and well after his usual time—we were tucked away in a private dining room at the Diogenes Club in Pall Mall, a few doors down from the Carlton. It was an undistinguished building that one could easily pass unless given explicit instructions as to how to find it. For its members—"the most unsociable and unclubable men in town," as Holmes had once described them—that was a great part of its attraction. He had also confided to me that Mycroft was one of its founders and that his brother was always to be found there from quarter to five to twenty to eight. It was now five twenty-three and my host was visibly edgy.

However, safely back within the embrace of its portals, Mycroft visibly relaxed and urged a

55

large scotch and soda upon me, which I was in no mood to refuse.

"I have taken the liberty of reserving a private room, Doctor, for the simple reason that one of the club's inviolable rules—which I am proud to say I steered through personally—is that talking is allowed nowhere in the premises with the exception of the Stranger's Room. And since the definition of 'Stranger' is a somewhat wide one and what I have to relate of the utmost confidentiality . . ."

He paused while a lugubrious and silent servant placed the food in front of us and left us alone.

"You will doubtless recall the name Bruce-Partington . . . ?" he said, his eyes fixed on the far wall of the room.

"How could I ever forget it?" I exclaimed. And instantly the events of five years earlier came flooding back. The secrets of Britain's ultra-secret submarine—the Bruce-Partington Plans—had mysteriously disappeared from the Woolwich Arsenal and Holmes and I had been called in by Mycroft on behalf of a petrified Government to bring them back.

"I fancied not." Mycroft took a sip of the excellent Montrachet he had ordered from his private stock and dabbed delicately at his lips with his napkin. I have often observed that the largest of men are among the most fastidious.

"At that time the Bruce-Partington submarine

was so powerful, so far in advance through its technology of anything else developed by other maritime nations that it gave our country an enormous, though as it turned out, temporary, advantage. To have lost that advantage through accident, gross error—or worse—would have been . . ."—he paused—"a pity." He managed to make that simple word sound more ominous than I would have thought possible.

"Fortunately, you and Holmes . . ."

"My dear fellow," I interrupted, "it was entirely your brother's doing. I just played a straight bat. It was Holmes who collared the bowling—if you see what I mean?" I finished lamely. I am never comfortable when people assign more credit to me than I feel I deserve. Come to think of it, though, Holmes did tell me the other day that though I might not be luminous, I was most definitely a conductor of light. Which I suppose he intended as a compliment.

Mycroft was now helping himself to a pinch of snuff from a tortoise-shell box and brushing away a few errant grains from his waistcoat with his red silk bandana. He absentmindedly offered the box in my direction but I raised a hand in refusal. I have quite enough reprehensible habits without embarking on another.

"As you wish, Doctor, as you wish. The fact of the matter is that, whoever *saved* it, the day was saved. But days have a habit of turning into months and years and, alas, the territorial imperative does not stand still to suit our convenience. Whichever of our 'competitors' hoped to purchase the Bruce-Partington Plans—and we have a pretty fair idea of who that was—was most certainly thwarted but only for the time being. In many ways the frustration fuelled their ambition.

"Today German sea power—for there is little point in beating about the bush, it is our 'distant relations' across the North Sea of whom I speak—their power is increasing exponentially. We—Her Majesty's Government believe, I should say—that it is her clear ambition to displace Britannia as ruler of the waves and particularly the waves that separate us from the mainland of Europe . . ."

"But the whole idea is—is . . ." I spluttered, almost spilling my wine.

"Inconceivable?" Mycroft completed for me. "Which is precisely why so few of my Lords and Masters . . ." and he managed to invest the phrase with quotation marks—"are prepared to take it seriously. Such things are not 'done' in polite society. And yet our sources tell us beyond reasonable doubt that the investment young Kaiser Wilhelm has made in his shipyards in the last few years far outstrips our own. Much of that output is lying in what my naval colleagues choose to call—somewhat fancifully—'mothballs' but it is there none the less and the building goes on apace. Admiral von Tirpitz has his express orders to make this a top priority. Meanwhile, the diplomatic pleasantries continue unabated. A genteel tea party in the parlour . . ."

"While someone is quietly constructing a bomb in the cellar?" I added bitterly.

"Quite so, Doctor, well put. A very fair analogy, as I would have expected from a literary man."

A thought struck me. "But what about Bruce-Partington? Don't I remember people saying that naval warfare would be impossible within the radius of its operation?"

"Indeed you do. But there was, I fear, an element of exaggeration in the claim, such as our technical fellows are inclined to make in their enthusiasm and, in any case, the technology involved has come on apace. Which brings me to today's events . . ."

I suddenly realised that here we were, comfortably ensconced in the heart of London's clubland, chatting about matters of state over which I, at least, had not the slightest influence, while London's mortuaries held the chilly corpses of three men brutally murdered—for what? And by whom?

Mycroft was now selecting a cigar with the care a woman might devote to choosing one priceless diamond over another. He continued . . .

"I mentioned that many of my 'colleagues' do not wish to face the facts of our situation. The story of the Three Wise Monkeys frequently comes to mind—but I digress. Fortunately, the Prime Minister is not of their number. For some time now he has covertly encouraged the development of what I might call Bruce-Partington II under the code name 'Phantom'— a submarine so advanced that not only can it outrun and out-manoeuvre anything the Germans have so far on the drawing board but it can operate at any depth with virtually no possibility of detection. It is aptly named for it will haunt our opponents' worst nightmares."

"But the three dead men. Were they spies—or what?"

"Anything but, I'm afraid, Doctor, anything but. No, those good fellows were on our side. They were a small group who worked together and called themselves The Good Companions. It was their little joke because of all the enforced time they had spent together. Montague, Pettigrew and Phipps—their real names, by the by—were the key design team for *The Phantom*. Each was a specialist in one particular area of the new technology . . ."

"So they were killed for the plans?"

"Nothing so simple, I'm afraid. None of them had any physical plans—we weren't going to fall into *that* particular trap again. What they knew was in their heads and no one piece of it was any use without the rest and even the sum of all three would not provide the whole picture. No, Doctor, these deaths are a shot across our bows, if I may drift into maritime parlance. Someone is telling us that our little secret is no longer secret and that nothing and no one is beyond their reach."

"But what about *The Phantom* itself?"

"That, I must confess, does concern me considerably. There is as yet only the one prototype. We have it undergoing final sea trials at a location I would prefer not to disclose for the moment even to you, Doctor. Should the forces behind these recent outrages manage to tamper with or even destroy that prototype, it would be a setback as much of time as anything else to reconstruct. And time, as you will have gathered by now, is of the essence. But more to the point in the current climate it would be a severe blow to national morale—one from which it might be impossible to recover. And however hard we might try to conceal them, the facts would inevitably emerge."

Fascinating as all this undoubtedly was, it paled beside the question that was consuming me as I sat there. Dusk was now falling and Mycroft's insistence on complete privacy had meant that no one had yet come in to light the gas lamps. My host was now a large blur, occasionally and fitfully illuminated by the glow from the end of his cigar.

Finally I could contain myself no longer.

"But what has all this to do with Holmes?" I cried.

"Possibly everything. Possibly nothing," was his inscrutable reply. "Oh, forgive me, Doctor, I have been treading the corridors of power for too long. A straight question receives an oblique answer as a matter of course. The honest answer is that I wish I knew. As you know better than anyone, my brother and I tend to commune without actually meeting very often. Both of us value our personal space and, truth to tell, we are not especially easy companions—perhaps we are too alike for comfort . . ."

I remembered on those few occasions that Holmes had ever referred to his elder brother, his admiration, though understated, had been profound. Mycroft's powers of observation he believed to be superior to his own. "Again and again," I can hear him saying, "I have taken a problem to him and have received an explanation which has afterwards proved to be the correct one."

"I had begun to alert him," Mycroft continued, "to some of my more cosmic concerns and I fancy I discerned the stirrings of interest . . ." In my mind's eye I suddenly saw the familiar Commonplace Book open at the entries on Germany. "Frankly, Doctor, I might have taken the conversation a little further a little sooner, had I not become exceedingly concerned—as I

CHAPTER SIX

...osedly we each of us dream every night ... lives but, if we do, I can rarely rememb... the following morning—perhaps because ...olmes is always telling me, I lack sufficien... ...ination. That night was an exception, ...ever.

...o sooner had I returned from that disquieting ...ning, I found (as I had anticipated) that ...mes had not returned and accepted Mrs. ...dson's offer of a "nice hot drink to help you to ...p, Doctor" than the effects of the day caught with me. I was asleep, my drink half finished, soon as my head touched the pillow.

The next thing I knew I was walking along ...e marble corridor of a portrait gallery. I was ...e only spectator and as I passed portrait after ...ortrait I began to realise that each of them was ...omeone who had featured in one or other of ...ur cases. There was Irene Adler (*the* woman) ...miling like a latter-day Mona Lisa, Sir Henry Baskerville, looking a little worried (as well he might), Jabez Wilson (his red thatch more like a wig), the murdered John Straker from the Silver Blaze affair . . . the hall seemed endless.

And then I realised that all the portraits were *alive* in their frames, smiling or scowling at me

66

know you are—about his increasing emotional volatility. He is not, I fear, the man he was before Reichenbach . . ."

"There is more than one set of falls for a man like Holmes," I concurred, sounding more like a homely philosopher than I had intended to be.

"Following his favourite dictum that once you have eliminated the impossible, whatever remains, however improbable, must be the truth, I would suggest, my dear Doctor that there are three possible explanations for recent happenings."

"And they are . . . ?"

"One. That the great Sherlock Holmes has been subverted to an alien cause and has committed these horrendous crimes in the mistaken belief that he is serving that cause.

"Two. That the accumulated stress of recent years has toppled his reason and that we are now dealing with an *alter ego* Holmes, a morbid clone of the man we knew."

"And the third?" I prompted.

Mycroft shrugged his massive shoulders and stubbed out his cigar with a sigh. "Just about anything else you care to devise, my dear friend."

We both rose to our feet. As I placed my crumpled napkin on the table and Mycroft rang the bell for the attendant, I heard myself say—"The first I cannot contemplate. The second . . . ?" *Could* I contemplate it? Could I

63

really? No, there had to be some other explanation, surely?

"So what do we do now, Mycroft?" I finished lamely. "Just wait?"

"I'm afraid we must indeed possess our souls in patience, Doctor," he replied, "but not, I think, for very long. There was one small matter I omitted to mention. Although the three victims called themselves The Good Companions, there were, in point of fact, *four* of them. The leader of the Phantom project and one of the world's most brilliant marine scientists is Harry Brotherton—a Yorkshireman and a died-in-the-wool one at that. Virtually impossible to winkle him out of his eyrie in the Yorkshire moors. The minute the project was completed, he flew back there like a homing pigeon. He now flatly refuses to go into hiding until the situation has been resolved. Consequently, we have put him under round the clock surveillance. Three down and one to go, one might say, and this time we are taking no chances.

"Under normal circumstances I would say that it was impossible for anyone to get near him—but then, these are not normal circumstances, are they?

"I would expect a report from my men some time tomorrow and I will keep you informed, Doctor. Oh, and one last thing . . ."

The door opened and the lugubrious servant

entered, his face looking, if anyt[...]
ever by the light of the candle h[...]
went around lighting the gas jet[...]
the details of the room, I felt as t[...]
slowly returning to the real world [...]
of time travel. But where had we be[...]

As Mycroft helped me into my coa[...]
"*A propos* our earlier conversation, [...]
a little gathering of like-minded sou[...]
afternoon at Westminster Hall. Two t[...]
have no more pressing engagement[...]
care to join me? It should prove enligh[...]

as I passed by. I swear from his expression that Grimesby Roylott was shaking his fist at me, although how that could be, when I could only see his face, was not entirely clear.

Then—rather like Alice—I had passed through a door and was standing in a park where two small boys were playing with boats in a pond. As one propelled his into the middle, the other would launch his on a collision course. Each of them had several and I noticed that one boy's boats were white, while the others were black. The first boy turned to look at me and he had the face of a young Mycroft. I tried to see the face of the other but somehow he would never turn in my direction.

And now I saw the figure of Holmes ahead of me. He was hurrying across the lawn towards another door that stood alone with no building to support it. He had closed it behind him before I reached it but it opened easily to my touch.

I found myself in a dark, empty room. Holmes was standing perfectly still at the end of it. Sensing my presence, he turned towards me. "Don't worry, old fellow, it's only me . . ." he said. As he spoke the last words, an identical image of him appeared by his side. "Only me . . ." The words echoed around the empty room and as they did so, image after identical image appeared, as in a fairground Hall of Mirrors, until the room was as full of them as the air was full of the sounds . . . *"me . . . me . . . me . . ."*

Then I felt a hand shaking my shoulder firmly but gently. I opened my eyes to find Mrs. Hudson standing over me.

"It's only me, Doctor Watson, but I thought you wouldn't want to oversleep. And Inspector Lestrade is waiting for you in the sitting room."

Waiting was perhaps not the right word to describe my visitor's behaviour. Pacing would have been more appropriate. So disconcerted was he that he had not even realised he was still wearing his shabby hat and coat as he gave a fair impersonation of one of the involuntary inhabitants of Regent's Park Zoo.

"Please be seated, Lestrade," I said, setting him a good example. "I gather there have been further developments?"

"I don't know if you can call them 'developments' exactly, Doctor," Lestrade answered, finally removing his hat and wiping his brow with a rather suspect handkerchief. "All I know is we've had three men murdered in less than three days—you've heard about the other one."

I nodded and he continued.

"Three men—Wilson, Roylott and Openshaw . . ."

Seeing me look at him questioningly, he corrected himself. "That's to say—Montague, Pettigrew and Phipps. Definitely connected they

68

were. Organised sort of fellows. Each of them kept a diary and, going by the initials, they all used to meet regularly at one place or another. Everything fits. They knew each other all right."

"Good companions, indeed," I thought, as Lestrade continued . . .

"Every time somebody who should know what they're talking about swears to seeing Mr. 'Olmes at the scene of the crime and each of those diaries has the initials 'S.H.' in 'em. Mr. 'Olmes himself has no explanation and now . . ."

"No Mr. 'Olmes—I mean Holmes?"

"That's about the size of it, Doctor. Now, if it was anyone else I'd have the lads combing the highways and byways." A rather bizarre image sprang to mind of a line of London policemen armed with combs. "But after all me and him have been through—and you, too, of course, Doctor," he added hastily. "But if he doesn't come forward within the next twenty-four hours . . . Well, I'm sure you can appreciate, Doctor, it'll be more than my job's worth. Forty years on the force next year and I can just see that pension slipping away. But there's got to be some simple explanation for it all, eh, Doctor? Tell me there is . . ."

The two explanations Mycroft and I had discussed the previous evening spring readily to mind but there was no way I was going to put them into words.

"Well, I just popped in to pay my respects, like—and to ask you to keep me posted personally, if anything *should* crop up. You can trust me to do the right thing, Doctor, I think you know that."

And, funnily enough, I knew that I did. Whatever his shortcomings Lestrade was as good a man as you would hope to find, no matter how long you looked. As he often said, he believed in hard work, not sitting by the fire spinning fine theories. Words failed me but, as he rose to leave, I shook him so firmly by the hand that he seemed a little surprised at the warmth of my salutation.

When he had gone I felt more than a little lost. This would never do. I had to hang on to some sort of normal routine until I could see a course of positive action. Holmes would never approve of someone just sitting around. Holmes would . . . So, of course, the first thing I did was to sit down. How could England—let alone the Empire—survive if a man was not permitted to read his morning paper in peace?

I picked up my *Morning Chronicle* from the neatly folded pile Mrs. Hudson had left next to my morning tea and settled myself in my chair. Routine, that was the thing—stick to a tried and trusted routine. It was the only restorative for sanity.

It was then that I noticed someone—presumably the newsagent—had scribbled something in pencil at the top of the page next to the banner. As far as I could make out the scrawl it said in large capitals—

ƎↃІЈA

I'm not much of a hand with foreign languages. What was it—Cyrillic or some eastern script? I determined to have a word with Mrs. Hudson when next I saw her. There was quite enough *about* these obscure foreign places in the paper itself without scrawling their mumbo-jumbo *on* the dashed thing.

Hm, things in South Africa were going from bad to worse. As I read the story, I recalled more of Mycroft's remarks from the previous evening. These damned Boers were being supported by German money and probably arms, too. Perhaps his theories were not, after all, as farfetched as they seemed. As I pondered this, I must have raised my eyes from the paper, for I found myself glancing at my reflection in the mirror opposite.

I saw a middle-aged gentleman of no great distinction and probably very little different from many who were sitting huffing over this identical newspaper at this very moment. Further inside several of them were quite likely to have letters signed—"Disgusted—Tunbridge Wells." That thought at least raised a smile with "Disgruntled—Baker Street."

And then I literally froze as someone dropped

an icicle down my back. For there in the mirror was a man with his newspaper, right enough. Except that the type was reflected backwards and the enigmatic

ƎϽIℐA

now read

ALICE

Alice! *The Alice In Wonderland Murders*. One of our most complex cases from a year or so ago. But why Alice and why now?

A thought was scrabbling around at the back of my mind, like a mouse behind a wainscot trying to get out. Alice . . . in the mirror. Alice—not in Wonderland but Through the Looking-Glass. A world where everything is the opposite of what it appears to be . . . a message that can only be read in a mirror.

I almost had it and then it was gone again. The mouse was silent behind the wainscot.

Before I could gather my fragmented thoughts again, Mrs. Hudson had entered the room bearing breakfast and a message from Mycroft confirming our afternoon rendezvous.

"You may not have been aware in your conscious mind but the decision was made for you by your *subconscious* mind, Doctor. This is the whole basis for my theory—for *one* of my theories. We are all—how you say?—'puppets' of psychological forces we do not truly understand, unless, of course, one has the benefit of a unique insight such as my own . . ."

The dapper little man seated beside me stroked his neat little beard to ensure that it was free from cake crumbs before he took another bite. To watch him demolish a Viennese *torte* in the very English dining room of Brown's Hotel had—I could not help but think—an element of coals to Newcastle.

It was only the second time I had had the pleasure of meeting the celebrated—some would say notorious—Dr. Sigmund Freud. A year or two before his *avant garde* insights had proved to be almost completely correct in the Shakespeare's Globe affair and since then his reputation had grown internationally in what I can only describe as a fitful series of leaps and bounds. Some said genius, others charlatan but few disagreed with his principal thesis that there were more things in the human mind than were usually dreamt of in our everyday philosophies.

Of course, I had known that the man was in London to launch his latest book; hadn't I read it in the paper? But I hadn't *really* intended calling on him when I happened to choose Brown's for lunch—or had I? Clearly, he thought otherwise. Why had I specifically chosen a table with a full view of the door and everyone who came into the dining room? Was it so that I could see or be seen? Why had I drifted into the reception at which he was signing copies of his book *On the Interpretation of Dreams* and picked up a copy? Was it because of the vivid dream I had just experienced or was I subconsciously trying to attract his attention? These are deep waters, Watson.

Wherever the tortuous path may have wandered, it ended with his standing at my table and giving a neat little bow from the waist. "My dear Doctor Watson, what a pleasant surprise—if, indeed, it may be so described. You are alone, I see. May one join you?" I indicated to the *maître d'* to pull up another chair and lay another place setting.

"No, no, thank you. You are too kind but I eat sparingly. Perhaps just a small pastry . . ." From the way the waiters bustled around it was evident that this was a regular occurrence and they knew precisely which pastries (plural) the little man had in mind. In no time at all he had a damask napkin tucked into his cravat and battle was joined.

Between bites he explained something of the latest controversy that surrounded him.

"You see, Doctor, it is abundantly clear to me—and you as a medical man will, I'm sure, appreciate this, although there are many qualified fools who do not—that in our dreams are to be found many of the keys to our motivation and our patterns of behaviour. The Theatre of the Mind, I like to call it. Not always literally, of course. Often the communication is coded, symbolised— for the symbol is often more potent than the object symbolised, is it not? For instance, that cigar you are about to light . . . is that really a *cigar?* Or is it really . . . ? But these are personal matters reserved for the consulting room and, besides, I am eating."

Which he again proceeded to do. While his mouth was so occupied, I could not resist the temptation to ask him something that had been on my mind all morning.

"Strange you should say that, Doctor, but I had a rather remarkable dream myself last night . . ."

Was it my imagination or did he lift his eyes skyward for a brief moment? I hurried on before I lost my nerve.

"I saw this image of—a friend of mine. But as I looked at him the image began to split up into many identical images, just as though I were looking at reflections in endless mirrors. What do you make of that?" I felt the pastry gave me an excuse to ask for a little something in return.

Freud paused and looked at me steadily, giving me the clear impression that he could see right through me.

"I make *la règle d'or*—the golden rule—never to hypothesise without being in possession of all the facts of a case . . ." How often, I thought, have I heard Holmes express just that very thought? In some indefinable way these two very opposite men had so much in common. What criminal could hope to stand up against the two of them? Then my train of thought was abruptly derailed as he resumed—

"However, 'off the record'—if I may so say—it would seem that you are concerned about your—friend. You worry that he is not completely himself, that he is perhaps 'coming apart.' Not the man you thought him to be? Through your own concern you fragment him. It is a common image of *angst*."

"But is it possible for one person to be *more* than one person?" I blurted it out before I could stop myself.

"More than possible, Doctor. In fact, quite common. You could almost say that each of us has several possible personalities that we manage to hold in balance. Consider even the most domestic scenario. One moment you are the adoring lover, next the gentle father, at others the stern employer and so on. Each is true and each a facet of you, which you allow to surface when it is appropriate . . ."

"What happens when it is *not* appropriate?"

Freud was concentrating on mopping up the crumbs on his plate but my question caused him to raise his eyes to meet mine.

"I think you speak of this 'friend' who splinters? Well, to be frank, there have been documented cases where the patient's personality appears to split down the middle, as if the person had been cut in half . . ." I shuddered involuntarily at his use of words. "The two halves then struggle for supremacy. Sometimes one is in the ascendancy, sometimes the other. And if one of them should have what we might call a negative motivation . . ."

He was now talking more to himself than to me and it was obvious that he was reliving old professional controversies. "There are many opinions on this matter and no one has yet found a suitable name for the morbid condition.

"Falvet—almost fifty years ago—called it *folie circulaire*, a typically ridiculous French conceit . . . Hecker called it *Hebephrenia*, Kahlbaunm wrote of *paranoia,* Kraepelin of *Dementia praecox*—all totally inadequate.

"Myself, I am more inclined to give it one name from the two key elements—the Greek words *schizein*, 'to split' and *phren*, 'mind.' Thus, *schizophrenia*. How does that seize your imagination, Doctor?"

Seeing that he had lost me somewhere in the middle of Ancient Greece, he concluded—"Wait and watch, my friend, wait and watch. Of course, Freud will not get the credit—but there is nothing new in that. One of my earliest precepts was—'A man may achieve anything—as long as he does not want the credit for it.' I have found this to be indisputably true."

Then with a sidelong glance at me, he untucked his napkin and went through the motions of a man about to depart.

"Have I answered your questions, Doctor? Ah yes, I see I have—but not perhaps in the way you were hoping. If I may offer a word of personal, as opposed to professional, advice it would be that I would try not to worry unduly about your 'friend.' He may have several images in your mind but, like the cat, he also has many lives. Oh, and please present my felicitations to Mr. Sherlock Holmes when next you see him."

He was almost out of the door when a final thought struck him. His last words could be heard by the rest of the room.

"Normally I would charge a fee but for a Viennese *torte* in this heathen isle, it is—how you say?—'on the houses.' "

CHAPTER SEVEN

Westminster Hall is one of those edifices—in which every capital city abounds—that smack to me of piety. Not piety of the religious variety—the Abbey across the way takes care of that—but there is something of the holier-than-thou about the crowds that flock in to celebrate some particular cause.

This afternoon was no exception. Big Ben was just striking the half hour as I made my way through the last minute stragglers approaching the Hall. Mycroft was ostentatiously consulting a large fob watch, which he stowed away in the recesses of his coat as I greeted him.

"Good man. Punctuality is one of my vices, I'm afraid, Doctor. Somehow I always feel I want to get my money's worth—even when the entertainment, as today, is *gratis*."

As he spoke it suddenly occurred to me that I did not have the faintest idea what the 'entertainment' was. Then, as we entered the vestibule, I caught sight of a large poster—

The
SOCIETY FOR ANGLO-GERMAN
SOLIDARITY
Special Meeting

President: Sir Angus McDoum
Guest Speaker: Klaus von Bork

"I do hope they repeat the name in full," Mycroft murmured as we entered the auditorium. "The acronym would be most unfortunate."

I took another look at the poster, which was liberally displayed throughout the room—S.A.G.S.—and had to agree with him.

I could now study the audience properly for the first time.

It was the usual rag tag and bobtail collection you can expect to see at any public gathering that does not charge admission. Overfed and slightly awkward looking couples from the shires; middle-aged ladies in undistinguished groups; minor clergy with a shine on their clerical black; a scattering of students.

All of this was perfectly to be expected but what did surprise me were the number of well-dressed men who looked as though the time of day would have mandated their presence at some City boardroom or in some other corridor of power. Here and there I thought I recognised a face or two from photographs in the more popular newspapers.

One face I most definitely knew was that of the man who was calling the meeting to order as Mycroft and I took our seats towards the back of the surprisingly crowded hall.

"So *that's* McDoum?" I whispered.

"Yes, and a somewhat disconcerting fellow he's turning out to be," Mycroft murmured back. "Backbench Independent M.P. for many a year for a safe constituency up on the east coast of Scotland. Westminster hardly saw hair nor hide of him from one year's end to the next. I doubt if more than half a dozen people could even tell you what he looked like. Then, in the last year or so he's popped up everywhere, talking about forming a Scottish Nationalist Party on the one hand—'Home Rule for Scotland' and all that . . ."

"Well, that's been bubbling for years . . ."

"Yes, but in the next breath he's talking about closer ties with Germany and how the northern Europeans must stick together against the 'Latin threat,' whatever that may be. I tell you frankly, Doctor, there have been moments in the last year when some of my 'colleagues' have been heard to wonder aloud if someone would not rid us of this turbulent laird? He really does seem sent to try us . . ."

A "Hush" from the row behind reduced us temporarily to silence.

McDoum was on his feet now, thanking us all for sparing our valuable time. However, he was sure that we would not consider that time wasted. We were, after all, contemplating the clean slate of a new century, the last of the present millennium. Time, surely, to assess both our personal and national priorities.

"Was it not the great John Donne who famously said that no man is an island 'entire of itself'? And, if I remember, he went on to say, 'Every man is a piece of the Continent, a part of the main' . . ." The man was in full stride now and I had to admit he was no mean orator. Donne's words came to life all over again. It was Mycroft's murmured aside that brought back my perspective.

"And if *I* remember, that particular quotation ends—'Never send to know for whom the bell tolls; it tolls for thee.' "

McDoum was now reminding us of the European "family" ties that bound us to our German relatives "in amity and fraternity."

"How long before he mentions *liberté and égalité*?" I whispered, drawing a snort from Mycroft and an even louder "Hush!" from the row behind.

Was the present enlightened ruler of a thankfully united Germany not the grandson of Victoria's eldest child, Victoria? And had he not married yet *another* Victoria, Princess Augusta Victoria of Schleswig-Holstein? If that did not suggest that stars were in alignment, he would like to know what did! (*Laughter*) But seriously, he wondered whether some of our own politicians could not learn a few lessons in application and consistency of purpose from Kaiser Wilhelm and his team, who had literally created a successful nation in a few short years, whereas we seemed determined to foster *dis*-integration of our own. (*Loud applause and cries of "Hear, hear!"*)

"A disintegration which you, my friend—wearing your other hat—are playing your own part in encouraging," I found myself thinking.

Having performed his role in warming up his audience, McDoum proceeded to introduce the guest speaker. Klaus von Bork was the scion of one of Prussia's leading families. He and his father were both close confidants of the Kaiser. His was the express portfolio to cement Anglo-German relations and today he would unveil a few of the exciting plans in prospect.

McDoum took his seat and I was able to study him properly for the first time without being distracted by what he was saying. He was a tall thin man somewhere in his middle to late fifties with a thatch of iron grey hair. The eyes, though deep set, were always in motion and clearly missed nothing. Even now he was scanning the room, like an actor-manager assessing how his play was being received by tonight's audience.

But when he turned briefly in profile it was his nose that caught my attention. Sharp and somewhat pointed, it resembled nothing so much as the beak of some predatory bird. Mycroft was obviously struck by a similar thought.

"Falstaff," he whispered. "And his nose was as sharp as a pen."

A small bell tinkled once in my head. I knew I had never met this man before but something about that face triggered an elusive association. I knew from experience it was no good pressing for the connection. It would come to me when it was good and ready and not a moment sooner.

Von Bork was speaking now. He might have stepped straight out of a Prussian cavalry regiment. Indeed, I learned later that he had done just that. In his late twenties or early thirties and arrogantly handsome in a cold, finely-chiselled way, he held himself rigidly to attention as he stood at the podium. His posture was in striking contrast to the relaxed message he was trying to convey.

He began by picking up on McDoum's "family" thought. Of course, we were family. Were not all the important royal houses of Europe merely *crèches* for our beloved Queen Victoria's off-spring . . . ?

Realising that this was intended as a Germanic jest, the audience—particularly the ladies present—laughed indulgently. Who, I wondered, had introduced that into his notes?

Oh—von Bork begged our pardon—he should, of course, have excluded our old friends in France from his statement about family. But then, we were all used, were we not, to the French and their eternal *différence*?

It was a shrewd touch and drew laughter and some applause. By touching upon the age old enemy we had been staring at, eyeball to eyeball across the Channel for centuries, he was by definition aligning Britain and Germany in the same camp.

Our two countries historically had always had much in common. Were they not both predominantly Protestant in religion? Let the politicians play their futile and irrelevant little games . . . (*Sustained applause*) It was time for the hearts and minds of the people of our great nations to have their say. After all, when the politicians were dust, the world would still speak of Shakespeare and Schiller, Beethoven and Bacon, Chaucer and Goethe—men of the mind. It was time to create a Community of the Intellect that knew no boundaries. Tomorrow—Great Britain and Germany. The day after? Why not One Europe? Was it *such* a demented dream? (*Cries of "No!"*)

As he went on to give details of the celebrated German singers, musicians and artists who would be coming over to their "second home" in the weeks and months ahead, I looked around me at the faces of his listeners. They were rapt. The ladies in particular seemed to be hanging on his every word and I reflected that it was probably no coincidence that this German "ambassador" happened to be young and handsome.

Now von Bork was listing the numerous art exhibitions and sporting occasions we could all look forward to. Finally, he came to his *pièce de résistance* or whatever the German equivalent happened to be. A leading German industrial company had graciously agreed to sponsor a comprehensive Wagner Festival at the Albert Hall with free admission for all as a gesture to the new spirit, etc., etc.

This last seemed to lack something of the impact he had clearly expected. Mycroft murmured that there was only one person of his acquaintance who would be likely to sit through *that*. Nonetheless, between them McDoum and von Bork had undoubtedly achieved their purpose. Their audience had heard what they wanted to hear, that there was an alternative and higher road forward, a magic wand that could be waved to charm their way out of what seemed increasingly like a downward political and social spiral. It was an impressive piece of applied mass psychology and I was beginning to see why Mycroft and his "colleagues" were concerned.

Ironically, I also recalled something one of the more xenophobic members of my club had said to me a few days ago when in his cups—"As soon as you take your foot off Johnny Hun's neck, you can expect him to bite you in the leg." Strangely, the two thoughts did not appear to be mutually exclusive right now.

Von Bork had resumed his seat and McDoum was on his feet again, asking for questions. As is typical on these occasions, many of these came from people who came to hear the sound of their own voices every bit as much as those of the speakers. Most would involve a preamble approaching a lecture with the actual question a mere appendage.

It was clear that what we were now witnessing was the usual British courtesy that was invariably meaningless on these occasions and I was about to ask Mycroft if we should not make our departure and anticipate the crowds, when something about the next questioner rivetted my attention.

I had noticed a number of clerics of various denominations among the audience and one of them was now rising, a little arthritically, to his feet. An elderly man, rather bent, with long snowy hair underneath his dusty black hat and a crumpled suit to match. He held on to the back of the chair in front of him for support.

I quickly scanned the platform and saw that McDoum, at least, was paying the reverend gentleman keen attention. Clearly this was not someone in the claque with which, I had no doubt, he had carefully seeded the room.

At first it seemed that we were in for a

repetition of the previous questioners. Did the distinguished speakers not agree . . . and then he drifted into some tortuous comparison between the aforementioned Shakespeare and Schiller and their religious views. Then—just as it seemed that McDoum was about to cut him off in full flow—the voice took on a different tone.

Gone was the rambling, high pitched clerical whine and a strong, clear and quite different voice enquired—"And I assume you both intend to take the requisite 64 steps to achieve your ends?"

I looked at Mycroft for enlightenment and saw a shocked expression that I'm sure matched my own. It was bemusement but behind it something more that I could not fathom. All around us people were looking at one another questioningly. Had the man lost his reason? What *was* he talking about?

Whatever it was, it clearly meant something to the two men on the platform. In a moment McDoum was on his feet thanking everyone for their patience and the sense they had conveyed of their intrinsic support for our "great cause." He hoped to see them again at any and all of the great occasions von Bork had so eloquently described. With that he declared the meeting closed.

Despite its anticlimactic ending, the gathering had certainly served its purpose for, as we left, the people around us were buzzing animatedly and appeared to have accepted the concept of our "German cousins" without demur. "That was a good one about the Frogs," I heard a ruddy complexioned older man say and it could easily have been my old club crony talking. Put in those terms, the "Little England" mentality seemed to lose a little of its charm.

Mycroft was clearly brooding about what he had just heard and, as we emerged into the late afternoon sunlight, delivered himself of his considered verdict.

"Cousins, brothers or whatever we may be beneath the skin, Doctor, but I tell you this—no German could ever have written *Hamlet . . .*"

"And why not, pray?"

"Because no German would ever let his hero be so damned indecisive." And he shook with subterranean laughter. Since no actual sound emerged, it was a quite remarkable sight to behold.

At that very moment I felt someone bump into me from behind. I turned to find the shabby cleric who had asked the strange question about the steps. Looking just as befuddled, he muttered an apology for his clumsiness, raised his hat and shuffled off into the distance.

"Strange fellow. I wonder . . ." I said, when Mycroft—his manner totally changed—grasped my arm.

"Check your pockets immediately, Doctor. I could have sworn he . . ."

I needed no further bidding, for I have a phobia about having my pocket picked. I thrust my hands deep into both pockets but, instead of finding anything missing, the fingers in my right hand pocket—the one nearest to the clumsy cleric—encountered what felt like pieces of paper. Quickly I pulled them out and found myself holding two theatre tickets for the Middlesex Music Hall.

Mutely I handed them to Mycroft, who turned them over and examined them as minutely as his brother might have done.

"You will note, Doctor, that not only are they for this evening's performance but that each of them bears one or other of our names. It would appear that someone wishes to entertain us and possibly enlighten us at the same time. I feel it would be churlish to refuse under the circumstances. After all, Sherlock is not renowned for his generosity . . ."

"You mean? *Holmes* . . . ?"

"I was fairly sure inside the Hall there. That absent-minded vicar has always been one of his favourite disguises but he is inclined to forget that some of us have studied his repertoire over the years. I suppose he felt that the filthy lascar—another of his predilections—might prove inappropriate for the context, for which we must be duly grateful. I did not think it germane to mention it at the time, in case it should interfere with whatever stratagem my brother has in mind. Perhaps this evening may do something to clarify precisely what that may be. *A bientôt*, Doctor—as our French non-cousins are fond of saying . . ."

And with that he handed me back one of the tickets and hailed a passing cab.

CHAPTER EIGHT

I t was a thoroughly discombobulated medico who let himself into Baker Street a little while later. So many different emotions were ricochetting through my brain that, after Mycroft's departure, I decided to walk home while I attempted to arrange them in some semblance of order.

So Holmes *was* somehow involved in this devilish German plot—but on whose side? And how did his appearance at the Hall fit in with his role in the recent murders—always supposing he was *involved* in the murders? What was the significance of the question about—what was it?—"taking the 64 steps"? And why had Mycroft made no subsequent reference to such a cryptic remark? By the time I reached that familiar front door I was no nearer coming to any conclusions.

I took my seat in my usual chair opposite Holmes's empty one, feeling rather as I imagine a solitary bookend must, and watching the daylight fade on the buildings opposite. How often had my friend and I sat thus, sometimes setting the world to rights, often in companionable silence? Had we—I wondered—done so for the last time? Was it all to end not in some heroic apparent fall over a cliff edge in an alien land but in domestic ignominy and disgrace for the greatest man I had ever known?

The thought so disturbed me that I found it impossible to sit any longer and found myself pacing the room. It was then that I noticed something was out of place. It took me a moment or two to determine what it was.

I had carefully replaced Holmes's commonplace book on the appropriate shelf when I had been consulting it earlier. Now the volume was clearly protruding, as if it had been pushed back in a hurry, yet Mrs. Hudson knew better than to interfere in this holy of holies. But who else could have replaced it? Had Holmes himself been here and . . . ?

I took the book from the shelf and opened it. Immediately it was clear to me that it had been tampered with. The magazine articles on Germany were still firmly in place but the biographical piece of—what was the fellow's name? Gruyère? Geier?—had been neatly cut out. All that remained were a few sharp paper edges.

I called sharply for Mrs. Hudson and within an instant, it seemed, that good soul was in the room. No, she most certainly *hadn't* touched the book, Doctor. Mr. Holmes was most explicit on these matters. Had Mr. Holmes himself returned in my absence by any chance? Of that she couldn't be certain.

"I'm so used to one or other of you coming and going at all times of the day and night, Doctor . . ." A slight exaggeration but I let it pass. "I really only take proper notice when the doorbell rings."

And there I had to leave it. One more question to add to my lengthy list. What might I have learned from the article that would shed light on these increasingly deep waters?

And talking of light, the next thing I knew was that I was sitting alone in the dark and clearly had been for some considerable time. I shook myself awake. Come, Watson, this is getting us nowhere. Faced with this situation, what would Holmes do now? Since I found even that question insoluble, I decided to resort to my own tried and trusted approach, which is to get up and *do* something. I took the ticket from my pocket, then went to get dressed for the evening ahead.

I have to confess that an occasional evening at the music hall is something that appeals to my plebian tastes. Much as I enjoy accompanying Holmes to a concert of classical music, I do so as much to please him as anything else. The sight of him, eyes closed in rapture and those long, eloquent fingers conducting in time to the music is often more entertaining to me than the performance itself—though those in adjacent seats have been known to indicate otherwise.

There are those who favour the New Oxford but for me there is no hall to touch "The Old Mo"—the Middlesex Music Hall in Drury Lane. I have won many a drink at the club from people trying to guess the derivation of the nickname and coming a hopeless cropper. For an old Indian man the association is an easy one. The place was originally called The Great Mogul after the Mogul of Hindustan, Aurengzebe (1658–1707)— now you see why I always win! It was a public hall supposedly frequented by Nell Gwynne— but, then, wasn't everything in that part of London?

Be that as it may, the neighbourhood is redolent with theatrical associations and, fortunately, I'd allowed myself ample time to ramble through it on my way to the hall. Kemble, Macklin, Garrick, Dryden—the names seemed to conjure up stentorian voices from the past as I wandered through the streets named after them.

Now I could see the gas jets outside "The Old Mo" and the crowds jostling to gain entrance. One of the things I find most pleasing about any of the great music halls is the way it serves as a melting pot for society. Working men and their ladies, certainly, but tinkers, tailors, shopkeepers, lords and layabouts, too. Add the odd courtesan and cutpurse and you have the Victorian equivalent of the old Elizabethan playhouse.

In the confusion of recent events I had omitted

to find out what the evening's entertainment held in store but a large placard soon provided that information. It appeared that we were to attend a Special Gala performance sponsored by—would you believe it?—The Society for Anglo-German Solidarity, the proceeds to go to the Cultural Liaison Fund, whatever that was.

Reading further, I had to admit that the organisers had gathered together a bill that would have made any commercial management envious. Whether the artistes concerned had the least idea of why they were appearing and the cause they were serving, I very much doubted. I had time to register the names of Dan Leno and Marie Lloyd, two particular favourites of mine, when I felt a tap on my shoulder and turned to find Mycroft towering over me.

The fact that he was wearing an opera cloak that would have comfortably housed three normal sized people caused me to wonder if he was truly in the habit of descending to the level of this mass entertainment. The accompanying thought was that the experience might do him—and the people he served—a world of good.

We were early enough to have time for a drink at the bar and, curiously enough, in the seething mass of humanity that made up the audience—a theatre in itself—Mycroft for once did not seem to attract undue attention.

As discreetly as I could I scanned the faces

for a glimpse of the shabby cleric but, though I detected several members of the cloth taking their pleasures with no apparent concern for their eternal souls, I could not see the face I was looking for. Not that I was particularly surprised. Holmes was not one to repeat an effect.

Which was not to say he was not somewhere hereabouts. I will always treasure the memory of his telling someone that he had been following them. "But I saw no one," the man replied—to which Holmes responded: "That is what you may expect to see when I follow you." In scanning this evening's crowds I saw everyone and no one. Did that prove the invisible man was here?

Then I became aware that Mycroft was talking to me.

"He will be here, Doctor, you may depend on it but the only thing I would wager on is that the dog collar is presently hanging from a hook in one of the many safe houses he maintains around the metropolis. What odds would you give on his being that Cockney fellow with the bowler hat and corncob pipe? Or that dowager lady with the pearls? No, I'm afraid we must wait until whatever plot he has devised is to be played out . . .

"Talking of which, our friend Inspector Lestrade visited me at the Diogenes just before I left. I must say that he looked a little quaint in context. Whispering does not come naturally to members of the constabulary, it would appear. However, he did manage to convey to me that his superiors have now concluded—after assessing the so-called 'facts' of the undoubted murders—that, unless Sherlock comes forward with some explanation of his own movements within the next twenty-four hours, they will reluctantly have to issue a warrant for his arrest."

"You can't be serious?"

"I'm afraid they are in earnest, Doctor. And disturbing as it may be, one can see their dilemma. Three brutal murders, which we know to be linked, and the only apparent clue a man who has been identified at the locations of all three and refuses to explain his presence. What else *can* they do?"

I was on the point of questioning him further when the sound of the pit orchestra striking up and the movement of the crowds in the bar indicated the entertainment was about to begin. Finishing our drinks, we moved into the smoky auditorium and took our seats, conveniently placed towards the back of the hall, so that we could survey the audience as well as the stage. What were we looking for? And how would we necessarily recognise it if we saw it?

I do not wonder that the French call their entertainments *divertissements*. It was not long before I found myself completely forgetting the cloud that hung over us and the purpose that had brought us to this unlikely spot this evening. The acts that had been assembled—apparently from all over Europe—were the finest of their kind and I should have hated to be the one to foot the bill for bringing them together for this one performance.

There was a French high wire act involving flaming hoops that defied description. At one point I found myself clutching Mycroft's sleeve, which seemed to amuse him immoderately. There was a Russian magician who seemed to carry a veritable aviary about his person and I could swear that at one point he had more doves fluttering around him than there are pigeons in Trafalgar Square.

The first half ended with Dan Leno, one of my perennial favourites. A small man, no more, I would have judged, than five feet two or three inches tall, he had the ability to take on the persona of so many different characters. Tonight he was playing a fireman of hilarious ineptitude but it mattered little what guise he chose. I had seen him as a railway guard, a shop walker and goodness knows what else but the lugubrious view of life remained the same. That downturned mouth told you that the cards of life were stacked against him and inanimate objects his sworn foes. You laughed with relief because all of his woes were not happening to you.

His command of an audience was such that by the time Leno was standing at the footlights chatting about the latest exploits of his fictitious neighbour, Mrs. Kelly—"She's started to advertise, you know. 'Young men taken in and done for.' "—I even noticed a muscle in Mycroft's jaw was starting to twitch. Now Leno went into his famous clog dance and the curtain fell to thunderous applause, marking the end of the first half of the entertainment.

"I wonder what *they* made of it all?" Mycroft asked, indicating a group of men in the front rows wearing German military insignia who were now ostentatiously lighting large cigars.

"They are probably comparing it unfavourably with the Ride of the Valkyrie," I answered a little sourly, for there was something about their proprietorial attitude that irritated me. Then it occurred to me that we were not here for the show itself but for some as yet undisclosed purpose of Holmes's.

Instead of joining the crush in the bar, we remained in our seats and scanned the audience. Since we had not the faintest idea of what we were looking for, it proved a barren pursuit and we were soon reduced to studying the programme for clues.

"You will notice, Doctor," Mycroft remarked after a few moments of doing so, "that the principal acts are almost evenly divided between English and German artistes."

"Indeed," I replied, "but let us hope we have heard the last of that fat German tenor who sang those endless drinking songs! Now, who have we to look forward to?"

Running his finger down the page, Mycroft stopped at one entry. "This might be interesting, Doctor. 'The Great Mysterioso—the Man of a Thousand Faces.' " He was now reading aloud from the programme notes. "Mysterioso is a recent recruit to Europe's thespian ranks. Before becoming an actor he was . . ."

I suddenly heard myself saying—". . . a diplomat?"

"Correct. But how . . . ?" Mycroft was turning to face me as much as his bulk would permit in the small theatre seat.

And in truth I couldn't for the life of me remember *how* I knew, except that it was in something I had read somewhere in the past couple of fragmented days. But before I could explain as much, the sound of the orchestra striking up the music for the second half made further conversation impossible.

As entertainments go, it was a strangely hybrid affair. Most of the individual acts were brilliant by their own lights but those that pleased the English regulars baffled the German contingent and those that set them on a roar left the rest of us cold. I felt myself thinking that what I was watching was a perfect paradigm for the whole putative "Fraternity." It was a concept based on a false premise. And then I remembered that those who were fostering it for their own purposes knew this perfectly well.

One act who did manage to fuse the disparate elements into one genuine audience was Marie Lloyd. Coarse of voice and disreputable in appearance, that little Cockney sparrow seemed to stand for just that humorous truculence that the stolid Germans would never understand, let alone appreciate. You can understand another nation's language word by word yet never have any true sense of the significant attitudes that made its people what they were.

Nonetheless, for the few minutes she was on stage "Our Marie" reached out and embraced each and every member of that audience with her personality. When she sang a saucy little song called "She'd Never Had Her Ticket Punched Before," her nods, winks and chuckles made her true meaning abundantly clear but her unashamed *joie de vivre* removed any trace of offence. By the time she invited—or, should I say, instructed?— us all to join in at the chorus of her closing song, there was not a person in that hall who did not do so wholeheartedly. I could even see the *meistersingers* in the front rows doing their best to have a good time.

Oh, Mr. Porter, what shall I do?
I want to go to Birmingham
But they're taking me on to Crewe . . .

A stentorian croak from my side told me not even Mycroft was immune from the lady. I glanced at him covertly and could only wish I could have somehow pinned down for posterity the sight and sound of him bellowing . . .

Oh, Mr. Porter, what a silly girl I am!

As Our Marie took her final bow to some of the loudest applause I have ever heard in a theatre, the German master of ceremonies—who had been alternating with his English equivalent all evening—came bustling on. I could almost hear some superior officer in the wings ordering him to get on and cut short the applause of the English *frau* before she steals the show, *nein*?

We would now have the great honour, he assured us, of seeing a performer of such magnificence that he was before the crowned heads of Europe appearing. Other artistes, however talented—and he made a belated bow in the direction Miss Lloyd had made her exit—had to be content with just one personality, but the Great Mysterioso . . .

I felt Mycroft tap my arm with his programme and I could sense a heightened tension in the air, although perhaps I was creating it myself. The purpose of the evening had to be revealed soon.

. . . The Great Mysterioso could count his in the thousands. Ladies and gentlemen, *mein herren und damen*, that excellent German entertainer, the Man of a Thousand Faces—The Great Mysterioso . . .

As he departed, the curtain rose to reveal a virtually empty stage, dimly lit. Seated on a simple chair his back to the audience was a tall slender man holding something in his lap. As he lifted it, one could see that it was a military helmet. He placed it on his head and turned to face us.

There was a collective gasp from the audience, for there in front of us was Kaiser Wilhelm II. There was the perfectly groomed military moustache, the haughty demeanour, the aristocratic stare—even the crippled arm held awkwardly at his side.

There was a moment's silence and then wave after wave of applause, led by the German contingent, several of whom leapt to their feet, a few even saluting. It was a remarkable likeness.

For the next several minutes The Great Mysterioso continued to amaze. Alone on the stage except for a wickerwork "property" basket, he performed entirely in mime. A voice from the wings would call out the next "subject," Mysterioso would turn his back on the audience, busy himself in the open basket and then turn to face us as an entirely different person. I studied him minutely—and I was conscious that beside me Mycroft was doing the same. The man had a plastic face, if that was, indeed, his real face and not another of his impersonations. I fancied that one could pass him in the street without his presence even registering—just like the thousands of people one met in daily life. Yet when he inhabited a given personality, as he was now doing to increasing shouts of "Ooh" and "Ah," he seemed to take on a whole identity. I was forcibly reminded of the way that Holmes himself disappeared into the recesses of another being when he adopted one of his own disguises. Not just the appearance but the very soul.

The very thought triggered off such a train of questions that I almost missed the next remark from the Master of Ceremonies who was himself having trouble making himself heard over the almost continuous applause.

"Ladies and gentlemen, *mein herren und damen*, in conclusion The Great Mysterioso will impersonate any famous person you wish to nominate. Just one name, if you please . . ."

"Sherlock Holmes!"

The voice came from my side. I turned to see Mycroft sitting forward in his seat, for it was he who had spoken.

There was a moment's silence, then a warm

round of applause. On the stage did I see Mysterioso hesitate for a moment? If so, the feeling of heady excitement any performer must enjoy when an audience is so audibly on his side clearly overcame any hesitation. He turned and began to rummage in his box of tricks, as the orchestra in the pit played a few anticipatory chords.

Then he straightened and turned to us in profile. I heard myself gasp. It was Holmes to the life. The same aquiline profile. The same thin mouth clenched around the stem of a meerschaum pipe.

The audience erupted in a storm of applause which would—I hope—have gladdened my friend's heart, since it demonstrated a genuine affection for the subject of this superb impersonation. Or *was* it an impersonation? I turned to Mycroft to see if he was sharing my thoughts but his face was totally impassive.

Then I realised that something was happening at the front of the auditorium. One of the German contingent was on his feet and staring fixedly at the stage. It was von Bork.

As if propelled bodily, the German Master of Ceremonies was now on the stage, thanking us for our reception of The Great Mysterioso, while behind him the curtain rapidly descended on "Sherlock Holmes."

From the other side of the stage emerged a troupe of clowns but whether they lived up to their programme billing of "Europe's Laughter Makers" I was not to discover, for Mycroft's hand on my elbow was propelling me towards the Exit.

"I believe we have both seen and observed what we were sent here to observe, Doctor. It now remains for us to decide precisely what that was."

A moment later we had left the world of illusion behind and were in Drury Lane, supporting actors in London's street theatre.

CHAPTER NINE

There must be something in the Holmes family genes that precludes conversation when it conflicts with cerebration. Sitting in that cab with Mycroft, as we bowled along towards Trafalgar Square and St. James's, I found myself looking at the very same expression I had seen on Holmes's face more times than I could count. The frozen countenance and the fixed stare totally belying the hum and whir of mental wheels turning.

The only remark he addressed to me was when he alighted at his lodgings. Tipping his hat, he thanked me for "a most illuminating evening." "Until we meet at Philippi, Doctor—wherever that may chance to be. But I fancy it will be soon." And then he was turning his key in the lock.

Whatever thoughts had been going through Mycroft's mind, I know my own was racing as the cab continued its steady progress to Baker Street.

What had we just seen on that stage? Holmes in another of his many guises? But for what possible purpose? Holmes as an associate of the German contingent—or was this his way of telling Mycroft and myself that he was *in* it but not *of* it?

The waters were not only getting deeper but they now threatened to engulf me.

That night I had a version of the same dream but this time I walked up to the mirrors. There were the multiple images of my friend's face and he appeared to be smiling at me encouragingly. But then, one by one, the faces melted and blurred and each became someone different. The three murdered men fought for possession of one face, each dissolving into the next and they were not smiling at all. Another became McDoum, who turned into von Bork.

I saw Lestrade turn into Mycroft, who then became the anxious cleric. I turned to the central image of Holmes for some explanation. "Don't worry, Watson," it seemed to say, "only a *thousand* faces. Well, perhaps a thousand and *one*." And then I found myself staring at my own face!

Only then did I realise that my nightmare had awakened me, so that I was sitting bolt upright in bed and looking at my own reflection in my bedroom mirror. With a sheepish smile at my tousled appearance, I immediately got up and started my morning toilet.

The next two days came close to making me feel I was losing my reason. I am like Holmes in that one respect. I cannot bear to be idle once the game is afoot.

And yet what was there to do? Holmes had vanished and, if anything, the mystery around him was deeper than ever. Clearly, he was offering up clues—or was one side of him sending out signals about the other? And were both of them trapped in the same body? I thought of my fellow Scot, Robert Louis Stevenson's macabre tale of the good Dr. Jekyll and the evil Mr. Hyde. But this was ridiculous—that was fiction. So what were *we* dealing with?

And what about Mycroft? So apparently forthcoming to begin with and now cloaked in a tent of silence. And as for Lestrade—I could imagine him and his men sniffing around like deranged bloodhounds without the faintest idea what trail they were trying to identify. For some reason the thought amused me immoderately and temporarily lifted my spirits.

I determined to occupy the time usefully, however long it might turn out to be. If Holmes needed me, he knew where to find me, as did Mycroft. Although I had now given up my own practice, I occasionally—when circumstances permitted—offered my services as a *locum* and, since the sick, like the poor, are always with us, there was plenty to keep me busy.

Thus it was that I was returning to Baker Street in the late afternoon two days later, keenly anticipating putting my feet up and relaxing over a scotch and soda with the early edition of the evening paper. Scarcely had I put my key in the lock when the door was opened for me and I found myself staring into the anxious face of Mrs. Hudson.

"Oh, Doctor Watson, I was hoping it was you. Inspector Lestrade's upstairs and he's been here ever so long. He seems very excited by something. I do hope there's nothing wrong with Mr. Holmes. There isn't, Doctor, is there?" Her voice followed me up the stairs, which I began taking two at a time, slowing down only as I approached the door of our sitting room. As Holmes has often emphasised, one must never go to Scotland Yard. We must let Scotland Yard come to us. Which Lestrade duly had.

He was sitting tensely in what I was pleased to see was the guest chair. Even though neither Holmes nor I had been present when he arrived, he was perfectly conscious of the proprieties in 221B. Mrs. Hudson was clearly correct about his state of mind, for he was twisting his bowler hat around in his two hands as though it were the steering wheel of one of those automobiles everyone is talking about.

I tried as best I could to control my own concerns but clearly the man had news to impart. "Well, Lestrade," I said in the sort of tone I hope Holmes would have used, "I assume there have been developments?"

"Lumme, Doctor, I should say so." And he

began to turn the brim of his hat rapidly in the other direction, a manoeuvre that would surely have spelled disaster on the highway.

"I should say there *have* been developments but as to what they mean, why your guess is as good as mine." Since there was no answer to his remark that did not involve either hypocricy or offence, I held my peace and let him continue.

"Ever since we pieced together the connection between those three fellers . . ."

"With a little help from Mycroft Holmes," I could not help but interject.

"Er—yes, the elder Mr. 'Olmes did give us a certain amount of assistance with our enquiries." Lestrade had trouble meeting my gaze. "However, be that as it may, and cognisant as we are of the existence of a *fourth* associate in a certain highly confidential venture, which I am not at liberty to discuss . . ."

Mainly because you know nothing about it, I thought uncharitably.

". . . we have had the said individual under constant surveillance and . . ."

"And?"

"I have just received this communication from the Yorkshire police under whose jurisdiction the said surveillance falls . . ."

"For heaven's sake, Lestrade, forget all the 'saids'—what does the message *say*?"

"Well, Doctor, the gist of it is that this feller

Brotherton is one of those stubborn Yorkshiremen who won't be told nothing—anything. There are the local police trying to keep a discreet eye on him, all for his own good and he . . ."

I could just imagine what a "discreet eye" meant in a small Yorkshire village on the edge of the moors. His every movement would be recorded and gossiped about from cottage to pub. I began to feel some sympathy for Brotherton.

"And he . . . what, Lestrade?"

"He insists on coming and going as normal, long walks over the moors and everything. Says everybody's worrying unnecessarily and the whole business is a load of stuff and nonsense— or words to that effect."

"What about his three colleagues?"

"Says he's sorry about them, of course, but implies they were soft southerners, whereas a Yorkshireman's an altogether different proposition. Bit of whistling in the dark to keep up his courage, it sounds to me, but there's nothing we can do to make him act any differently."

"Indeed, not, but get to the point, Lestrade. You're not here today because one gritty north countryman is refusing to do as he's told . . ."

"Quite right, Doctor, I'm not. If that was all there was to it, I'd keep my fingers crossed and hope for the best but the last couple of nights it seems there's been some strange goings on up at Humblethwaite . . ."

"That's the village where Brotherton lives?"

"Right you are, Doctor. Tiny little place right up on the edge of the moors. Couple of dozen houses and cottages, a pub—although they call it an inn—The Humble Wayfarer. Their idea of a joke, I suppose. And then there's this rather larger place set apart and actually on the moor itself. Used to belong to the local squire, when they had one."

"And now Brotherton lives there?"

"Lives there on his own with just a housekeeper. Holdover from the days of the old squire. She's the one that alerted the local police."

"Alerted them to what?"

"Strange noises around the house in the early hours."

"An intruder?"

"No, Doctor, that's the funny part. No sign that anybody tried to break in."

"Then what?"

"Just the curious business of the dog in the night time."

"What did the dog *do* in the night time?"

"Just kept howling. Brotherton said he hadn't heard a thing but she didn't believe him, she said. When he left that first morning for his walk, he seemed to pause a long time just outside the gate. When he'd gone, she went out to see what he'd spent so much time looking at. And what she found was . . ."

"The footprints of a gigantic hound."

"But, Doctor, how did you . . . ?"

"Never mind for the moment, Lestrade. Am I right?"

"Absolutely one hundred per cent, Doctor. Some great big dog had been prowling around and there may have been a man with it. The local police thought they could see footprints but it rained that day—it does most days up there, by the sounds of things—and they were pretty well washed out. Then, when the exact same thing happened again *last* night, they thought they were getting a bit out of their depth, like, so they sent for Scotland Yard." And here he self-consciously straightened his tie.

Then, like a raconteur who suddenly remembers he's omitted to tell the ending to his story. "Oh, I'm afraid there's one other thing. There's been a guest staying at The Humble Wayfarer these past two days . . ."

I paused for a moment, trying to decide whether to let the words pass my lips but we were too deep into this thing now and the truth must out, whatever it turned out to be.

"He is registered as Henry Baskerville and he answers to the general description of Sherlock Holmes?"

Lestrade was now giving an impersonation of a landed fish that would have won him a round of applause at the Middlesex Music Hall.

"Well, I'll eat my hat . . ." he said, apparently unaware that he had just dropped it on the floor. Then with a rueful shake of the head—"We hardly need Mr. 'Olmes when we've got you, do we, Doctor?"

Conscious of his *faux-pas*, he proceeded to blow his nose noisily in a none-too-clean bandana.

"Well, you know what I mean, Doctor. This here telegram came just in the nick of time, I can tell you. The Commissioner had come to the reluctant conclusion that we had to put Mr. 'Olmes on our official 'Wanted' list but I've managed to persuade him to hold his horses until I've looked into this little lot." And he held the telegram aloft for emphasis.

"I've taken the liberty of booking three seats on the Yorkshire express this evening. I thought you and Mr. Mycroft would want to be in at the— would want to see how things turned out? He says he'll meet us at the station. He's been called over to the Cabinet, I believe. Some national emergency requiring his attention, I shouldn't wonder."

A few minutes later Lestrade had taken his leave without pressing me further on my "insights." By now he knew me well enough to know that I would share with him any information germane to his investigation and we did have the prospect of a lengthy train journey ahead of us.

I was glad of some time to digest what I had just heard and to try and make sense of it.

Three brutal crimes had been carried out, all of them parodies of one of our more famous cases. Now here, it appeared, were the makings of a fourth, the *coup de grâce*. But there was one important difference here. All three of the previous cases had been published and their details—or such of them as I had chosen to reveal—were in the public domain. But while there had been partial and discreet news reports of the dramatic events that took place at Baskerville Hall back in 1889, I had so far—at Holmes's insistence—refrained from publishing my own account of what I considered our most successful case, which I intended to call *The Hound of the Baskervilles*.

Outside the files of Scotland Yard, only Holmes and I were privy to the details. A chill ran through me as the implications of that thought struck home. Almost as a reflex action I hurried over to the writing desk where I am in the habit of keeping my notes. One entire drawer was stuffed with the manila folders that hold the details of past cases that, for one reason or another, have had to be withheld from the public. Quickly I riffled through them.

The names scribbled on the covers in my medico's scrawl—some of them a little faded now—brought memories flooding back. "The

Amateur Mendicant Society," that luxurious club hidden in a furniture warehouse . . . "The Camberwell Poisoning Case" . . . "The Lighthouse, the Politician and the Trained Cormorant," a story no one would ever believe! . . . "James Phillimore," the mystery of the man who stepped back into his house to fetch his umbrella and was never seen again—a puzzle that vexed Holmes to this day . . . and, of course, "The Giant Rat of Sumatra," a story for which, in my judgement, the world will *never* be prepared . . .

And, ah yes, there it was—"The Hound of the Baskervilles." I pulled it out from the pile and opened the folder. It took only a moment for me to realise that the pages had been disturbed. I am a reasonably tidy sort of fellow, a result, no doubt, of my army training and to retain some semblance of order in what is by now a considerable mass of material, I am in the habit of securing the separate manuscripts with ribbon. I did not need to be Sherlock Holmes to detect that this ribbon had been untied and refastened by hands other than my own. So, when I looked more closely, had several other packets.

But whose hands could they be but Holmes's own?

Mrs. Hudson would die rather than tamper with anything so obviously private. But then, so would my friend. Over the years he had made it a point never to read my accounts until and unless I insisted he do so prior to their being published in the *Strand*. In point of fact, he was wont to criticise my efforts more often than he would praise them, claiming that I was bent on putting what he called "colour and life" into the narratives instead of sticking to the pure logic of the reasoning from cause to effect that he considered to be the essence of the cases. When I assured him that I had no intention of boring my readers to death and that the human emotions were every bit as germane to the story, he would simply shrug and pick up his violin. His own form of retribution, I have often thought.

So why would Holmes now wish to study what I had written, unless . . . ? Unless Jekyll had finally yielded the stage to Hyde?

Sadly I replaced the folder and locked the drawer. Was I looking for the last time at the fragile mementos of our life together?

Just over an hour later I found myself sitting in the corner of a carriage on the Yorkshire Express with Lestrade opposite me. The train was already five minutes late but there was some excitement at the ticket barrier which was clearly holding things up.

Then, like the Red Sea, the crowds parted and Mycroft emerged, sailing calmly down the platform like a ship of state, a frock coated young man struggling along in his wake under the weight of a large portmanteau.

Soon he was sitting opposite me, looking more like a graven image than ever. I judged that whatever business had taken him to Downing Street, it continued to weigh on him, so I did not press him. I knew him well enough by now to realise that he would convey whatever he felt I needed to know in his own way and in his own good time—and not a moment sooner.

Lestrade, who is not entirely an insensitive man, clearly felt the tension and tried to relax it a little.

"Well, well," he said jovially, rubbing his hands. "How does that bit from Shakespeare go? *'When shall we three meet again/In thunder, lightning, or in rain?'* "

Since it happens to be one of the few quotations I can ever remember from Shakespeare or anyone else, I couldn't help adding . . . *"When the hurlyburly's done . . ."*

Which brought the response from Mycroft—"A most appropriate sentiment, gentlemen, were it not for the fact that the three of us have already met. The local weather forecast for the Yorkshire area does indeed prognosticate thunder storms for this evening and, as for the next line of the quotation, I believe it runs . . . *'When the battle's lost and won . . .'* Since we are facing a battle which I have no intention of losing, I shall—if you will excuse me—attempt to keep my powder dry."

And with that, he tipped his hat over his eyes in a gesture I had seen Holmes himself use many a time, and appeared to fall sound asleep.

CHAPTER TEN

The weather was indeed as dour and unrelenting as one might expect from the home of *Wuthering Heights*—a book I had once read at Holmes's express suggestion and found unbelievably depressing. "Yes, but that is because you invariably read for the element of romantic fiction," he had replied crossly when I mentioned the fact. "Trash, I grant you, but look at the underlying study of morbid psychology. It could only have been written by a woman." A remark I *still* consider to be somewhat ambiguous.

The brooding presence of the Brontes seemed all around us as we were spirited along in the pony and trap Lestrade's local colleagues had arranged to meet us at the nearest station. Soon we had left the town behind and were trotting along in open countryside.

The storm that had been forecast had so far held off but it had begun to rain, that hard driving rain that finds every chink in one's clothing and leaves you feeling utterly bedraggled. All of us had been wise enough to dress for the occasion, for in my experience the weather in this part of the world is unreliable at the best of times and this was most decidedly verging on the worst of times. Nonetheless, despite my sturdy ulster and sensible boots, I was feeling distinctly vulnerable to the elements and I could sense that my travelling companions, too, were missing the accustomed convenience of city life.

The trap was being driven by a member of the local constabulary delegated to meet us. He was a grizzled veteran of many summers and rather more winters, to judge by his appearance, and I would have been prepared to wager that in all those years he had never been called upon to investigate any crime more serious than a little light poaching. He introduced himself as Sergeant Micklem.

"Well, Micklem, any developments since your cable?"

Lestrade's tone was authoritative—one might even say officious—now that he was dealing with one of his own, as he saw it.

Even at this distance the long arm of Scotland Yard clearly impressed the locals. Micklem was anxious to assure his London colleague that no stone had been left unturned in their untiring efforts to provide the service required. "But if only t'lad would stop still," he lamented. "He's got round heels, that 'un."

Brotherton, it transpired, was a fresh air fiend and forever tramping the moors outside his house, despite all warnings. Moreover, he refused to allow anyone to accompany him on his perambulations. "Mind, I noticed he took a fair old stick with 'im today, like, so mayhap he's seeing a bit o' sense at last." But Micklem's flat lugubrious tone filled none of us with any great confidence on that score.

"Other than that, then, there's nothing new to report?" Lestrade asked.

Micklem was shaking his head when I asked— "Has Brotherton *missed* anything in the last day or so? Some personal article?"

Micklem paused for a moment's thought, then replied—"Funny you should say that, Doctor Watson, but his housekeeper did say that he was complaining he couldn't find one of his favourite old gloves. And it can get a mite parky up on these here moors."

It was the answer I had fully expected but my heart sank within me. It was the curse of the Baskervilles all over again. The would-be murderer, the wretched Stapleton, had purloined one of Sir Henry's boots from his hotel room in order to give the "hound" its victim's scent. Brotherton's glove, I feared, was intended to fulfil precisely the same function.

Mycroft and Lestrade exchanged puzzled glances but, for the time being at least, refrained from questioning me further in front of Micklem.

A little while later we pulled up outside The Humble Wayfarer, where Micklem had reserved rooms for us. By this time the first fingers of the storm had reached us and the sky promised worse to come. The rain was falling steadily and there was the rumble of distant thunder. Every now and then the sky would be lit up with a flash of distant lightning that increasingly threatened to move in our direction.

Inside the inn was the welcoming sight of a blazing fire and the landlord and his wife had clearly taken great pains to welcome these strange southern beings. Anxious not to offend them, I assured them that nothing would please us more than to enjoy a hearty meal by their fireside and that we would assuredly do just that, once we had paid a courtesy call on our friend Mr. Brotherton.

This produced a raised eyebrow on the part of the landlord. "Happen you'll find him out at this time."

Mycroft indicated the sound of the wind and the rain that was even now gusting at the door of the inn. "In *this* weather?"

"Oh, we breed 'em hardy in these parts, sir," the landlord replied with a smile, "and *that* one . . ." he gestured in the general direction of Brotherton's house—" 'e don't take no tellin'. Anyway, gents, we'll have something tasty for you when you return."

"By the way," I said as casually as I could, "I don't suppose my friend, Mr. Baskerville happens to be in?"

"A friend o' yours is he, sir? No, he's been out

all day. We don't see a lot of him, do we, my love?" He looked at his wife who nodded her assent. "Keeps pretty much to himself does Mr. Baskerville."

Nature never loses her power to surprise and remind us how puny are our powers compared to hers. As we struggled in the direction of Brotherton's house, the wind turned us into crouching primeval figures, fresh from the cave. Whatever dignity we might wish to think we could command on our home turf, here we were reduced to *homo* with precious little trace of the *sapiens*. I'm sure each of us was wondering what we were doing here but there was no opportunity for conversation of even the most rudimentary kind. It was all we could do to concentrate on reaching our destination.

Fortunately, the bulk of Mycroft forging ahead provided some degree of protection and I must have resembled nothing so much as the page to Good King Wenceslas, as in my master's steps I trod, fervently wishing to exchange the wind and rain for a little snow lying "deep and crisp and even."

After what seemed like hours—but could only, in reality, have been ten minutes or so—we were plying the iron knocker on the door of a solid but plainly built house set right into the edge of the moor. Behind us on the way we had come

y had the reverberations of his words
 vay—for the crags created a natural echo
 er—than we heard a sound which struck
 he marrow, for I had heard it before under
 stances I hardly dared to recall.

 s the cry of one of the Hounds of Hell.
 nstant later I saw a sight I had hoped
 to see again. High on the cliff edge was
 rton struggling with a huge dog that was
 g on its hind legs. The moon chose that
 nt to emerge from behind the scurrying
 and throw the pair of them into relief,
 t as if they were characters battling at the
 of some old melodrama—except that this
 appening right in front of our eyes and was
 real.

 two combatants, evenly matched for height
 veight, struggled in total silence, while the
 of us on the ground below them were rooted
 spot . . . It must have been an unearthly
 au.

 denly I came to my senses and cursed
 lf inwardly. What was I thinking of? My
 ce revolver! Thank heaven my instincts had
 me to bring it. It was the work of a moment
 rieve it from the pocket of my ulster, cock it
 ake aim.

 onsider myself a pretty fair shot but now
 ed two real problems. With fragments of
 d, shredded by the storm, scudding across

we could still see the occasional faint light of some dwelling but before us was nothing but the darkness of the abyss, or so it seemed.

The door was opened by a wisp of a woman, elderly and frail but still bright of eye. I recalled she had been here most of her life, staring out at the moor and listening to its secret voices. She hustled us inside in a trice and before we knew it were sitting before a roaring fire with a hot drink in our hands.

Mrs. Platt—as she introduced herself—had been a widow these many years. She and the late "Mister" (God rest his soul) had worked for the old squire for donkey's years. Oh, she could tell us many a tale and almost certainly would, had not Mycroft—by one of these pieces of diplomatic *legerdemain* which had secured his reputation in the corridors of power—managed to divert her smoothly to our present purpose.

Mr. Brotherton? A fine gentleman, to be sure, though not to be compared with the old squire. Why, she could remember . . . Then, catching Mycroft's eye, she made a fair summary of the events of the past few days, which we listened to as politely as possible, since it was clear we should hear nothing else until this chapter of her narrative was complete. In all respects it tallied with what we already knew—with one addition. Her employer, she had the distinct impression, was *afraid* of something but of what she could not say.

And where was Mr. Brotherton now? "Oh, heavens above, you just missed him. He went out for his late night constitutional a moment before you arrived. If I hadn't been prattling on you'd have surely caught up with him on the edge of the moor but he'll be well into it by now." And she proceeded to give a detailed itinerary of Brotherton's routine. He was, it appeared, a man of regular habit in these matters, which was some small consolation for the delay.

Once again we braved the night and the elements. As he opened the solid front door, it was almost torn from Lestrade's hands. A moment later we heard it bang behind us like the clap of doom—to be immediately echoed by a peal of thunder.

"It's not a fit night out for man nor beast," Lestrade shouted above the noise of the wind, then seemed to realise the incongruity of his remark and said no more.

Despite the housekeeper's detailed directions, it was impossible to know how closely we were following Brotherton's tracks. Even as we walked, the rain was filling in our footprints and blinding us. Then I noticed that, while Lestrade and I were blundering along, Mycroft seemed to have developed a definite sense of direction. It was almost as if he could divine by a broken

branch here, a displaced clump Hard
path our quarry had taken. died a

Deeper and deeper into the m chamb
and then—even more dramatic me to
begun—the storm suddenly ceas circun
found ourselves at the epicentre It wa
be engulfed all over again at any An
as it may, the effect could not never
dramatic if it had happened at Broth
Opera House in the middle of *Go* standi

The three of us looked at one an mome
have said "thunderstruck" but th cloud
longer appropriate. The curtain of almos
and I could now see that we we clima
among a series of precipitous cı was l
indeed fortunate that one or other all to
fallen and injured ourselves getti The
such utter ignorance of the terrain. and v

"There he is!" It was Lestrade, p three
silhouette of a man standing some to th
away on a flat rocky bluff. Hearing table
man turned in our direction, as sui Su
us as we were relieved to see him. mys

"That's Brotherton, right enough," serv
to me. "Thank heaven we are in tii told
Then, raising his hands to his moutl to re
trumpet, he called out. "It's all right, and
it's me—Mycroft Holmes. Just com I
join us. Everything is under contro I fa
chap." clou

the moon, the light was constantly coming and going like the flame of a flickering gas jet. Then the struggling figures above us moved to and fro, as though engaged in some ghastly minuet. Nonetheless, I knew time was running out for them and for me. Any moment the dog might gain the mastery and then it would be all up for Brotherton, as it so nearly had for Sir Henry Baskerville all those years ago.

And then I saw my chance. As the moon shone out with momentary clarity, Brotherton—with a last superhuman effort—managed to slip his partner's embrace, leaving it pawing at air. Before I was conscious of doing so, I had loosed off a shot. There was a single terrible howl and the beast disappeared from our view.

Brotherton was now on his hands and knees at the very edge of the crag, exhausted by his efforts. I was aware of Lestrade rushing to and fro in an attempt to find a path up to him. How badly had I incapacitated the hound? Was it about to attack again? If so, Brotherton was no longer in a position to defend himself further. The need to reach him was urgent.

And then the fickle moon cast a shadow on him. But this time it was not his four footed assailant. This time it was the figure of a tall man with a pistol pointed unwaveringly at the scientist's head—the figure of Sherlock Holmes!

I heard Mycroft gasp beside me and I was

conscious that I myself was holding my breath, as if to exhale might break the tension.

Then someone spoke—above us and to our right.

"*Was ist da los, mein Herr*? Or perhaps I should say—'Would you please be so kind as to drop your gun and stand well back?' "

All our eyes—Brotherton's included—turned to the direction of the voice. On the top of the opposite crag stood the mirror image of the man threatening Brotherton. Ulster billowing in the gusty wind, the familiar deerstalker that was his invariable country wear. The only unfamiliar aspect of his appearance the revolver aimed at his *doppelgänger*.

I never expect to see a sight like it if I live to be a hundred. If this were a game of chess, then at that moment we were all in check.

And then the "first" Holmes made a false move. The arm with the pistol wavered, uncertain whether to aim at Brotherton or the newcomer. In what could only have been the merest fraction of a second, he clearly decided to change his target and the gun began to move from the perpendicular towards the horizontal.

A shot rang out, the pistol spun from his hand and landed at my feet, and Sherlock Holmes—or at least, his living image—was clutching at his useless shoulder.

The echoes of the shot were still dying faintly

132

away before Mycroft, Lestrade or I could bring ourselves to move a muscle. And even then it was that familiar voice that brought us back to reality.

"Gentlemen, if you would care to walk some twenty yards to your left, I think you will find a reasonably dry path to the summit. While I don't believe our flatteringly-garbed friend has any more pressing engagement for the moment, it might be as well to assure him that we would value his continued company—under certain conditions, of course."

The weight of the previous days fell from my shoulders and I literally bounded up that path like a two year old—with, I have to say, my two companions not far behind me. At the top a most bizarre sight greeted my eyes.

A bemused James Brotherton, his breathing laboured and his appearance, not surprisingly, disheveled, had his arms wrapped tightly around the pseudo-Holmes. The fact that the pressure thus exerted was causing the man to wince in some considerable pain appeared to concern him not at all.

As the first on the scene I now had the opportunity to study him properly, while keeping my service revolver at the ready for any unforeseen developments.

Certainly the fellow was approximately of Holmes's height and general build but, to my surprise, the face now in repose was almost bland. I was reminded of a blank slate. You could pass this man in the street and be quite unable to describe him afterwards. I was conscious that this was the second time in recent days that thought had crossed my mind. The eyes that he raised to meet my gaze were flat black pebbles, totally dead. I did not know this man yet I had the strongest impression that I had met him before.

Then a familiar voice broke into my reverie.

"Ah, Watson, I see you have made the acquaintance of Herr Klaus Geier, sometimes known as The Great Mysterioso . . ."

And then, of course, it all came flooding back. The Old Mo . . . the Man of a Thousand Faces . . . the fleeting but uncanny impersonation of Holmes that clearly disconcerted the German contingent. I still found myself grasping for pieces of the jig-saw but the general picture was coming into focus.

Holmes was in the forefront of the group that now joined us and we greeted each other warmly, my friend wringing my free hand in both of his in a rare display of emotion.

"How good to see you, old fellow. And you, too, Mycroft . . . Lestrade. I trust this evening's events will have satisfied even your taste for the theatrical. I must confess I thought the storm was a little overstated. I suspect even your most loyal readers will have a little trouble with the coincidence, Watson, but no doubt you will find a suitable way to couch your narrative so as to integrate it acceptably."

Brotherton had now recovered sufficiently to find his voice—a rather flat Yorkshire tone. He also appeared to recognise Mycroft. "I suppose I should thank you folk for what you've done and, believe me, I do. But will someone please tell me what the blazes is going on?"

Before anyone else could answer—even supposing they could have provided him with an explanation—Holmes moved forward to take charge of the situation. Consigning Mysterioso, who now looked something less than Great, to the safe keeping of Lestrade, he drew us over to where the dog lay and knelt at its side.

"Careful, Holmes," I cried, "the creature may still be dangerous!"

"I rather think not, old fellow. Come, take a look." I moved gingerly to his side and peered over his shoulder. Seen at close quarters, the animal was nothing like as terrifying as it had appeared earlier.

"Why, it's only . . ."

"A reasonably large male Alsatian—which I believe out American friends have the prescience to call a 'German shepherd.' Luckily, you only appear to have inflicted a slight flesh wound."

"Luckily?"

"Indeed. After our little affair with the Hound of the Baskervilles we shall be getting into the bad books of the Royal Society for the Prevention of Cruelty to Animals, if we continue to go around massacring their clientele. No, this is an ordinary domestic animal, almost certainly borrowed for the duration and of a perfectly docile nature."

"But the gigantic footprints?"

Holmes reached down to the dog's paws, gently unfastened something and handed me a glovelike arrangement shaped like an oversize foot. "The dog was given a set of these—just as a man might wear a pair of shoes larger than those he normally wore in an attempt to convey the impression he was someone else.

"A study of the prints, however, would undoubtedly reveal that the animal's weight was unevenly distributed with the pressure concentrated on the centre of the tread."

"But we saw it attack Brotherton . . ."

"No, you saw it rear up at him—a habit large dogs will indulge in when they get wind of some favourite scent. Brotherton's glove, you will remember, disappeared some little while ago and, unless I miss my guess, has been used to condition the animal. Perhaps the use of a little raw meat rubbed into the grain and—yes, I thought so . . ." He pulled at Brotherton's sleeve rather roughly. ". . . the jacket has been tampered with, too. There was no way the dog would fail to approach our friend here and, however friendly its intent, no way its 'victim' could fail to misread its intentions. Brotherton here was, in reality, evading its excessive affections."

"How do you explain the unearthly barking, though?"

"I think the explanation for that lies with Herr Geier. The Germans have long been known for their mechanical ingenuity and—here we are . . ." He moved over to where Geier was nursing his wounded shoulder, delved into the pocket of the ulster identical to his own and brought out a small box-like contraption with a small key in one side. As he turned it, it was obvious that it was a music box of sorts. I started involuntarily at the sound I had heard earlier—the demented baying of that Hound from Hell.

"The effect was all and—as might have been expected from our thespian friend here—it served its purpose well enough on anyone prepared to suspend their disbelief . . ."

I seemed to sense an implied, more in sorrow than in anger, criticism beneath the words and a covert glance showed me that the point had not been lost on Mycroft or Lestrade. Holmes might just as easily have said—"Oh, ye of little faith!"

"The theatre was intended solely to continue weaving the web of deceit that would tie me hand and foot in the deaths of Brotherton and his colleagues. The 'Hound' here . . ." and at this point his narrative was strangely interrupted by the said animal sitting up and licking Holmes's hand—". . . was intended as nothing more than a symbol . . ."

"Like the red wig or the orange pips?" I cried, seeing daylight at last.

"Precisely, Watson. If you were to look further in Geier's pocket, I don't doubt you would find the ligature with which he intended to strangle Brotherton. A neatness of mind that, in another context, might be considered quite admirable."

There was a clattering behind us and a small group of uniformed men emerged on to the plateau.

"Ah, yes, I had almost forgotten. When you left in your natural haste, Lestrade, you omitted to inform the local officers of the law of your likely whereabouts, so I took it upon myself to do so on your behalf. And now, as I notice the rain seems to have decided that we have enjoyed respite enough, I suggest that we leave them to tidy up here and remove ourselves to The Humble Wayfarer where, I have reason to believe, the landlord has a late supper waiting for us."

CHAPTER ELEVEN

Well, Sherlock, now that we have indulged you in your own version of theatre, perhaps you will be good enough to indulge us by filling in some of the gaps in our understanding of recent events?"

It was Mycroft, his usual composure completely restored, booming from the depths of the chimney corner. Lestrade had gone off with the local police to ensure that his prisoner was placed safely under lock and key. Brotherton had been restored to his own home, where his housekeeper repeatedly insisted that his bedraggled condition was the clear consequence of going out without his warm gloves.

The landlord and his wife had evinced no apparent surprise that a second "Mr. Baskerville" had replaced the first and appeared happy to answer to the name of "Holmes." Presumably they put it down to the inscrutable ways of these barbaric southerners.

The dog, his graze cleansed and bandaged by my own fair hands—in the absence of an available local vet—was now snoring comfortably in front of the fire, its head resting proprietorially on my left foot.

"The general drift was always clear to me, of

course," the elder Holmes continued. I could, had I chosen to, taken issue with him on that assertion but I decided not to. His speciality, after all, was supposed to be omniscience. "I assume the ball of thread began to unravel when I alerted you to the doings of SAGS?"

"Even earlier than that, brother mine, but not by much." He paused to light his favourite briar. "Your warning simply brought a certain coherence to various rumblings I was hearing from what I might term the undergrowth of the underworld. The Irregulars . . ."—he was referring to the Baker Street Irregulars, his loyal troop of urchins who, by virtue of their appearance and youth, could flit undetected through places where an adult would draw attention—"had been bringing me an increasing number of reports of unusual comings and goings on the part of certain suspicious individuals, people who normally were unconnected but suddenly seemed to have acquired common interests. And in many of these transactions the names of McDoum and von Bork recurred with monotonous regularity. Your briefing merely provided the magnet that attracted the iron filings to a common centre.

"Unfortunately, *my* attention attracted *their* attention. The people with whom we are dealing are formidably organised, gentlemen, and—as we have seen—entirely ruthless. I flatter myself they saw my possible intervention as, at the very least, an impediment to their grand plan—with which you, Mycroft, had been good enough to make me somewhat familiar. Hence their decision to use the one man who might credibly discredit Sherlock Holmes . . ."

"Sherlock Holmes?"

"Thank you, old fellow. Modesty would have prevented me from completing the thought. Yes, if they could persuade the powers that be that someone they had reason to trust implicitly had either been suborned or turned rogue elephant, at the very least they could create a distraction for an administration that can hardly be said to be united on this or any other issue of the day. If Sherlock Holmes is thought to be abroad, busy *creating* problems, he can hardly be trusted with *solving* them!

"It was, I must admit, an unexpectedly subtle stratagem for the Teutonic mind to come up with the idea of using my own cases to implicate me. In fact, it is my surmise that an Anglo-Saxon intelligence is at work there—possibly the enigmatic McDoum. We shall see . . .

"It is, I must confess, a little disconcerting to find oneself face to face with—oneself."

"But Holmes, how did they know so much about you—the pipe, the tobacco . . . ?"

"Elementary. For that, Watson, I believe we have your liberally detailed accounts of our domestic life to thank . . ." There was an emphasis on the use of "thank" that I chose to ignore. "But it was when I ascertained that the 'evidence' was not simply a fair likeness but actual objects of mine that I began to take our opponents seriously. Someone out there was able to impersonate me well enough to gain access to Baker Street and deceive even those who knew me well—such as Mrs. Hudson and yourself, old fellow. Your story about my not remembering where I kept my pipe convinced me of that."

"You mean that was . . . ?"

"Mr. Dopple . . . or, since German seems to be the fashionable language at the moment, Herr *Doppelgänger*—a 'supposed spectral likeness or double of a living person.' After you were good enough to warn me . . ."

"But I didn't know *myself,* Holmes!" I protested.

"You warned me all the same, Watson—for which I am in your debt. After that I employed my somewhat unorthodox resources and soon located my nemesis. After which, I became *his* nemesis. Since that small *contretemps* at Reichenbach it has been my habit to establish a number of what I might term 'safe houses' around London. In each of them I keep certain changes of identity. My dear fellow, have I omitted to mention the fact? Then I am even deeper in your debt.

"In one of them resides an amiable non-

142

conformist clergyman. In another a somewhat disreputable lascar seaman . . ."

Mycroft and I exchanged impenetrable expressions.

"Mr. Dopple was observed and occasionally accosted by several of my 'friends' as he went to and from his normal place of business. My old bookseller—you remember him, Watson?"

How could I ever forget him? It was the character in which Holmes had reappeared in our rooms after his "death" at the Reichenbach Falls. When he let the mask fall, he had been the cause of my fainting clean away and I had neither forgotten nor entirely forgiven him for it but that was another matter. Holmes continued oblivious, carried by his own narrative.

"My old bookseller managed to sell him a dog-eared copy of *Das Kapital*, which he deposited in the nearest bin when he thought I was out of sight. Probably just as well. I doubt that his lords and masters would appreciate its sentiments under the present circumstances.

"The Great Mysterioso. Also known as Klaus Heinrich Geier. Civil servant turned actor. Acclaimed by the crowned heads of Europe for his unrivalled ability to impersonate anyone— just as he has impersonated me these past few days and, since it was hardly likely that I could expect him to pose in my company to demonstrate the point, I had to bring the two of us together for your benefit on the stage of that rather disreputable music hall. My dear Mycroft, I do beg your pardon for offending your sensibilities in that way . . ."

Mycroft raised a dismissive hand to render the apology irrelevant and I could have sworn the eyelid turned in my direction drooped slightly in what might in an ordinary person have been a wink.

". . . and by the way, had you not called out, I was poised to do so myself. I had gambled—correctly, as it turned out—that the vanity of an actor in command of an adoring audience and with the adrenaline coursing through his veins cannot resist the temptation to show off. Geier momentarily forgot his real purpose when the whiff of the greasepaint was in his nostrils."

Another piece of the puzzle clicked into place in my brain.

"Alice. Alice in the Looking Glass. That was your way of telling me . . . ?"

"That things were not as they seemed, old chap. Correct. That, in point of fact, they were the mirror image of the way they appeared. It was a reference that would only make sense to one man in the entire world, after the adventure we shared so recently. And I knew you would be anxiously looking for a sign."

I nodded—I hoped sagely—and hid my blushes in a copious draught of the local brew.

"Other than his enviable ability to lose his own identity—supposing he has one—in that of someone else, I fear Herr Geier is a rather stupid man. To go to such pains and then apparently forget that he is *left-handed* . . ."

"The *marks* he left?" I interrupted.

"The marks, indeed, and the knotting of the 'speckled band' in Pettigrew's case. Both clearly the handiwork of a *sinister* rather than a *dexter*, as I would have thought was obvious even to someone like Lestrade. However, it seems that the more exotic indications can so easily overwhelm the obvious.

"For instance, the individual letters on the notes were clearly cut out and stuck down by a left-handed person. You will have observed that a left-handed person *pushes* the pen across the page, whereas a right-handed one *drags* it. In the same way the marks made by scissors show similar differentiation of pressure. Then a partial fingerprint in the paste on Pettigrew's note indicated the thumb print from a left hand. That thumb bears a small scar, which mine—as you see—does not. Truly pathetic! The man might as well have signed his own name."

It was Mycroft who now interrupted. "And, of course, Mysterioso held the pipe in his left hand in the music hall. Which, of course, is what removed the final doubt in my own mind."

I looked at that impassive face. I strongly

suspected that he was being economical with the truth but years of practice in his professional capacity stood him in good stead and I did not choose to pursue the point. Then an inspiration struck me.

"Oh," I said casually, "it came to me a little earlier than that. You remember that Hungarian juggling act in the first half? The Scarlet Hussars? Five brothers dressed entirely in red— red tunics, red boots, red wigs? It was when I noticed that one of them didn't have his wig that I said to myself—'Montague' . . ."

Two pairs of identical gimlet eyes bored in my direction but by then I was busy tamping down my pipe. Two can play at that game.

Reaching forward to stir the fire into life, Holmes continued his narrative.

"Having satisfied myself that I now knew the melody of this little *intermezzo*—for it is nothing more in the greater scheme of things—I knew I had to play it out. My inexplicable and continued absence would force them to continue. My sense of it is that they had expected to entangle me in the meshes of the law after the first three murders. Nonetheless, they believed their plan was foolproof, no matter what. One more dramatic murder and Sherlock Holmes would be a hunted man with a price on his head.

"Moreover—and I do not believe I flatter myself when I say this—the furore so caused would effectively divert attention from their real plans, a part of which I believe, Mycroft, you have already divulged to Watson here?"

There was an assenting grunt from the depths of Mycroft's chair.

"So the *fourth* man had to die—and die in a fashion more lurid and newsworthy than the others. But which of our cases would fulfill those requirements? Once I discovered that Brotherton was a man of the moors, albeit the *Yorkshire* moors, I knew at once what the answer must be. Our little adventure on Dartmoor.

"Taking advantage of your absence, my dear chap, I referred to your notes of the affair—and, frankly, I have to admit that this is your finest work. Why you have waited so long to put it before the public, I cannot imagine. But I digress . . . When I unearthed them . . ."

"You found someone had been there before you?"

"Exactly so, Watson. And clearly someone other than your good self. You have the invariable habit of aligning the top of the sheets of your manuscripts and setting the ribbon exactly in the middle of the pile. Our avid reader was not so meticulous. He also tied a left-handed knot—but let me not belabour that childish error. Nonetheless, all of this only confirmed my own intuition as to the direction of the next move. It was a simple matter to make my way up here in advance of Geier, take a room in the next village as 'Jas. Grimethorpe—Commercial Traveller. Ladies' Haberdashery' and then wait for 'Sherlock Holmes' to arrive. Or 'Sir Henry Baskerville,' as it turned out. A casual word with the local constabulary over a convivial drink in the bar here—Sergeant Micklem, I believe is the man's name—and I could be sure that word would reach Lestrade. I'm afraid I was guilty of embroidering my account, since up to that point the dog had, so to speak, done nothing in the night time. However, I felt a certain artistic licence was called for and I did . . ."—Holmes bowed ironically in my direction—"have a certain grasp of the plot.

"The rest, I believe, speaks for itself. And here to speak for himself is the admirable if slightly damp Lestrade." And he turned to lighting his own pipe with a brand from the fire.

And indeed, the Inspector did present a sorry figure, as he removed a coat turned black with water and squelched his way across to the fire, where he stood letting the steam rise from him. In the flickering firelight I thought he looked like one of the minor demons from Dante's Inferno. Then, remembering his dogged and unfailing support over so many years, I slapped myself on the mental wrist for my uncharitable thoughts.

Geier—Lestrade reported smugly—was safely under lock and key and would be transferred to London at some point that suited our convenience. For as long as we wished he would conveniently vanish. Under the circumstances no one chose to mention *habeas corpus*.

"I've told Micklem and his lads that, if they want to stay the right side of Scotland Yard, their lips are sealed as tight as—a drum," he added, mixing a rather curious metaphor. "As far as they're concerned, nothing that happened tonight happened until I *say* it happened. If you see what I mean, gentlemen?" he ended lamely. We assured him that we did indeed.

While Holmes and Mycroft gave him a suitably edited version of the events we had just been discussing, I went into something of a brown study as I attempted to digest what I had just heard.

So von Bork and McDoum and whoever else was involved in their infernal plan had hoped to kill at least two of the proverbial birds with the one stone? Not only would implicating Holmes in a murder trial distract his attention from their affairs, thus allowing them to proceed unimpeded with whatever they next intended, but it would positively aid their cause.

I think I can be reasonably objective about Holmes and, for all his irritating failings, he is a significant figure in the daily life of our country—a sort of hero, in a way, trusted to save the day when more conventional means have failed. To have that confidence undermined in such a dramatic way would certainly play into the hands of those who were arguing that our society was breaking down and that it was time to take drastic measures.

Now that we had Geier in our hands, the psychological advantage seemed to be moving our way for the first time. The enemy would be anxiously awaiting his report and his assurance that Holmes was duly bound hand and metaphorical foot—an assurance they would not receive. The Great Mysterioso would have mysteriously disappeared without trace—his greatest trick yet.

The playing field was momentarily level. But what happens next?

I must have inadvertently spoken the last words aloud, for Mycroft answered them for me.

"I think *I* may be able to throw a little light on that, Doctor."

CHAPTER TWELVE

Mycroft fixed his unblinking gaze on his brother.

"Steps," he said.

"Sixty-four, I believe," Holmes replied.

"Of course," I added. "I knew there was something else I'd meant to ask. That was what the vicar—I mean, that was what you said at the meeting. But what *are* the 64 steps?"

I might as well have been talking to thin air or to myself as the two verbal fencers thrust and parried in search of an opening. Every sentence was pared to the quick.

"A leak?"

"Land records."

"Inevitable."

"Elementary."

"Will somebody *please* tell me what's going on?" The anguished plea was my own.

With one final stare—which was returned in kind—Mycroft now encompassed the room as a whole.

"Forgive me, gentlemen, but I had assumed that I was one of the only three people—other than those occupied *in situ*—to be the possessor of that particular piece of information. I see I was misinformed. A fact which exacerbates the situation somewhat and will certainly force our hand to some degree.

"Doctor, I owe you an apology. When we dined together, I exercised a little editorial discretion in my account of recent events. I trust you can perhaps understand my motives?"

I grunted non-commitally and he continued.

"However, recent events now make candour obligatory. When we were looking for a safe location for *The Phantom*, my colleagues at the Admiralty undertook a most thorough search and finally settled on a remote location on the eastern coast of Scotland. They found an ideal spot which nature had sculpted from the base of some inaccessible cliffs, forming a natural harbour which is completely submerged at high tide. And, since the state of the tide is irrelevant to a submarine's peregrinations, it made the perfect temporary home for our purposes. Indeed, it proved to be so from every point of view—except one . . ."

"And that was?" I could not help but ask.

"Our neighbours. I should perhaps explain that the cliffs in question are adjacent to a small privately-owned island and linked to it by a set of steps carved out of the living rock . . ."

"The 64 steps!"

"Precisely, Doctor. The Admiralty negotiated a highly satisfactory lease with the owner—an arrangement the efficacy of which has only latterly been called into question. The question having to do entirely with the emotional state of our landlord."

"Who is?"

"Sir Angus McDoum."

Several proverbial pins could have dropped into the ensuing silence. Lestrade—to whom much of this was news—was staring mutely from face to face like the spectator at a tennis match anxious to gauge the score.

"Not that McDoum knows the precise purpose of our being there but the fact is that we have become uncomfortable bedfellows. The McDoum we first did business with was the man I described to you earlier, a vague and amiable recluse. The public figure you see today is like some reborn Christian zealot and a most uncomfortable neighbour. Fortunately, our lease is due to run out in a matter of weeks, at the end of the month, in fact, and our trials are virtually complete but—I must be frank with you, gentlemen—the proximity makes me nervous and yesterday's developments give me even greater grounds for concern . . ."

Now it was Holmes's turn to come to life. He leaned towards his brother and a falling ember from the fire caused a sudden flame to case a giant shadow over him on the wall, making him appear to hover over the room.

"And what happened yesterday, pray?"

Mycroft pondered for a moment, as if debating

how much he should reveal, then pressed on.

"Yesterday the Prime Minister sent for me privately to discuss a secret report he had had prepared unbeknownst to the rest of his Cabinet colleagues, many of whom—as I indicated to you, Doctor—do not share his concerns over recent 'developments.' "

He turned to Holmes. "The Sons of Albion?"

"A group of recent origin, reputedly drawn from all levels of society who believe it is their bounden duty to take the law into their own hands if the elected authorities are unable or unwilling to do so. They believe extreme violence to be the best purgative for what they perceive to be the country's present ills . . ."

"The end justifies the means?" I murmured, almost to myself.

"Something of the sort, old fellow, something of the sort."

"Our agents report that cells are being set up all around the country, though no one can suggest who is behind them or who is supplying their not inconsiderable funds and, quite probably, arms. That an organising mind is at work is beyond doubt—as is their purpose. In the overall scenario I outlined to you over dinner, Doctor, the Sons of Albion will be the *agents provocateurs*. They will be depicted in the media as the 'voice of England' speaking for the little people and crying revolution . . ."

"Let them shout their heads off," I cried angrily, "the British people will never be gulled by such nonsense."

"Don't be too sure of that, Watson," Holmes interposed. "The British people are probably less cohesive as a group than at any time in our recent past. They sense their effortless control of events, both at home and abroad, to be slipping away and they want someone to blame for that. The Sons of Albion will express their frustration in dramatic terms without their having to lift a finger in anger themselves."

Immediately the classic counter argument occurred to me. "They may tear something down but what will they leave in its place?"

"They will not need to leave anything. The work of reparation will be done by others. Our German cousins—in the spirit of familial fraternity—will offer to send us 'peacekeeping forces.' On a purely temporary basis, of course. They will even offer interest-free loans to fund extra 'security measures.' They already have enough friends in high places who will regard this as an offer they cannot refuse . . . and so the process will begin."

"*What* process?" I cried. I could not believe what I was hearing.

"Why the process of colonisation, Watson." Holmes spoke gently, as if to a sick child.

"Once in place, the forces would stay in place,"

Mycroft continued. "Those highly organised German 'helpers' would restore law and order but, of course, there would be no question of their leaving while there was a danger of further outbreaks. And since there would inevitably be further outbreaks in other locations, further 'helpers' would be needed, until . . ."

"But this is monstrous!"

"No, Doctor, it is much more insidious, because they would not be invaders but guests, here at our invitation. Then we should see the inevitability of gradualness at work. For many of our fellow citizens it would be like returning to the comfort and safety of the nursery. Things *would* be better organised. Somebody else would be fighting our battles for us. It would be a comfortable, thoughtless existence being a part of the German Empire—a little boring, perhaps. And a generation later, who would remember it had ever been any other way?

"Yes, there would be a Resistance movement, certainly—at least to begin with—and I would say our 'cousins' are counting on it, even relishing it as a form of exercise, something to keep their men sharp and on their toes. Good practice for the annexations to come, where the subjects are not so accommodating and supine."

"I think we would be deluding ourselves to think we can count on too much help coming from across the Channel," Holmes added. "What we prefer to think of as our effortless superiority is seen by many of our European neighbours as insular arrogance, I'm afraid. They would be only too content to see us receive what they would consider our comeuppance . . ."

"Stew in our own juice," Mycroft added rather surprisingly. "No, the plan is seductively simple. Which is why it must be stopped. Our fellow citizens must never be allowed to hear the siren song. Better to wait and face the declared enemy—for it will surely come to that before long—than to have to deal with the enemy within."

"Men will fight for a hope, however forlorn. Only a fool fights for a cause already lost." Holmes was staring into the flickering fire and seemed to be communing with himself.

It was the least philosophical of us—Lestrade—who shattered the mood with a practical question.

"Well, gents, what are we going to *do* about all this? We can't just *sit* here . . ."

The other three of us exchanged somewhat sheepish looks. Of course, he was quite right. It was this excess of introspection that made Mycroft's scenario ring too depressingly true.

"Quite right, Lestrade—the voice of reason. Action this day," said Holmes as he threw another log on the fire, causing the flames to leap and illuminate the room anew, as though a gas lamp had suddenly been turned up full.

We had been sitting in some nether region of the mind but now we were back in the real world. Four men who might have in their hands the ability to save the land they loved from an ignominious fate or—if they did not act decisively and effectively—be responsible for writing *finis* to centuries of courageous independence. What *were* we going to do about all this?

Mycroft was speaking again.

"It is our opinion—the Prime Minister's and mine—that the Germanic sense of theatre will incline them to wish to start their campaign, if I may so designate it, with a dramatic event—rather than starting with a series of apparently random happenings which then appear to escalate naturally. I further believe that the elimination of Mr. Sherlock Holmes—which they assume they have achieved this evening—neatly closes a particular chapter in their preparation . . ."

"But they *haven't* eliminated Holmes," I interjected.

"True. They will not receive the report they expected as soon as they expected it, Watson," Holmes replied, "and this will undoubtedly puzzle them temporarily. However, we now hold that particular card, since I am reasonably certain that Geier acted alone. Consequently, we shall hold them in suspense for a little longer. Already their nerves are stretched a little taut.

Our friends are not comfortable when there is a departure from their libretto and they clearly found the 'interruptions' at both the rally and the music hall disconcerting, to say the least. It is *my* belief, my dear brother . . ."—and he addressed himself to Mycroft—"that for all the reasons you have articulated—and for several others that need not detain us at the moment—our friends will advance their plans. The dramatic event, whatever it may be, will be sooner rather than later."

Mycroft looked more than ever like a graven image as he answered.

"Would Sunday, October 1st seem to you a suitable date?"

Now he had everyone's undivided attention.

"One other fact the Prime Minister wished to discuss with me yesterday was the intelligence he had received that the Anglo-German group—specifically McDoum and von Bork—have suddenly announced a top level symposium. It is to be held on that date in the presence of specially invited journalists from the world's most prestigious newspapers. Oh, and a *very* special 'special guest'. . ."

He paused a moment for dramatic effect.

"His Royal Highness, the Prince Edward—the man likely to be our King and Emperor within the foreseeable future."

Holmes and I exchanged glances.

"And I am told," Mycroft continued, "that HRH, despite the Prime Minister's most urgent advice, has indicated his willingness to attend *because* of the 'family connection.' "

He paused like an actor waiting to deliver his guaranteed exit line.

"Oh, and perhaps I should mention the venue. Castle Doum. Home of The 64 Steps."

"But this could be just the occasion those devils are looking for," I exclaimed. "Holmes, what are we to do?"

"An excellent question, old fellow. For myself, I intend to return to London. Moors do tend to have a certain repetitive quality about them, I find. Then I shall take tea with two new friends of mine . . ."

"Friends?"

"Yes, two gentlemen called McDoum and von Bork. They will be expecting a report and The Great Mysterioso has one more performance to give . . ."

CHAPTER THIRTEEN

H olmes and I took the train back to London on our own the next morning. Lestrade stayed to make arrangements with the local police for Geier's safe keeping. For the time being, the man simply ceased to exist. In due course, Scotland Yard—with Holmes's help behind the scenes— would piece together the evidence from the three London crimes and charge him but that would have to wait for another day. A trial, even *in camera*, would alert the enemy and this was a time when the element of surprise was our strongest suit and perhaps our only one.

As for Mycroft, a telegram had brought a carriage in the early hours that had whisked him off to some undisclosed destination. He was gone by the time we came down for breakfast, leaving a cryptic message—"Until we go to meet our Doum!—Mycroft."

As the train rattled its way south I took great comfort from the familiar sight of my friend sitting in the opposite corner of the carriage, his head wreathed with the smoke from his pipe.

So absorbed was I in trying to put the events of the last twenty-four hours into some semblance of order that I did not at first realise that Holmes had spoken. His gaze remained fixed on the countryside flashing past the window as he said—

"Watson, I owe you the humblest of humble apologies. Believe me, I am well aware of the strain you have been through since this sordid business began."

"Nonsense, old fellow, understand perfectly," I answered gruffly, also taking an inordinate interest in the rather nondescript Midland scenery. "Only thing you *could* have done under the circumstances."

"Good old Watson. Ever the pragmatist. You are the sharpening stone that gives me my edge. Forgive the rather prosaic analogy but I depend on you rather more than you know . . ."

Then, as if realising that these were indeed deep waters for a relationship based on years of unspoken understanding, he continued— "Once I had a faint understanding of the web being woven around me, it was vital that our opponents—whoever they may have turned out to be—believed that I was truly enmeshed, until such time as I could piece together the whole plot. To have challenged them too soon would merely have caused them to drop their plan and resort to some other stratagem, which we may or may not have discovered in time. By letting them believe they were succeeding, we have allowed them to go so far along their chosen path that they will be psychologically incapable of retracing their steps. They are a race dedicated to their own infallibility. With any luck it will be their eventual undoing.

"In persuading them that I had swallowed the bait, your reaction was key. Once I went underground, your behaviour was critical. They would be looking carefully to see how you reacted to the events as they unfolded. Oh, make no mistake about it, old fellow . . ." as he saw the look of surprise on my face—"you have been watched night and day ever since the Montague business and your obvious distress—for which, I assure you, I am duly grateful—was the confirmation they needed."

"Glad I could be of some use," I answered with somewhat mixed feelings. Then another thought struck me. That was all very well in the early stages but we had now crossed this particular Rubicon and there was no way back. The charade was surely over?

"But surely they will wonder when they hear nothing from Geier?"

"Ah, but they *will* hear this very day. I sent a cable from the station while you were buying our tickets. The Man of a Thousand Faces will face his paymasters at precisely 3 o'clock this afternoon. I have chosen the Café Royal. An ironic touch, I think you'll agree, since it is undoubtedly in their master plan to re-christen it the Café Kaiser."

"But Holmes," I protested, "why put yourself in this unnecessary danger?"

"Because, my dear fellow, it is the only way I can regain any degree of freedom. For McDoum and von Bork to believe that their plan has succeeded, the false Holmes has to reappear— or rather, the false Mysterioso. And besides, we need to know as much as possible of what they intend to do next."

"But how do you expect to convince them that they succeeded when we know that they did not?"

"Ah, but I don't expect them to take my unsupported word, Watson. But I wager they will believe an impeccable source . . ."

"Which is . . . ?"

But answer came there none, save a forefinger raised to the lips in the universal signal for silence. And he refused to discuss the matter further, continuing to gaze out of the carriage window until the train began to crawl through the dingy suburbs of north London and eventually arrived with a grateful sigh at King's Cross.

There a different man took over. Grabbing our paltry luggage from the rack, with a cry of "Come, Watson, no time to sit around woolgathering!" he hurried me out on to the platform.

"Over here, boy!" he called to a boy who was hawking the early edition of the evening papers. As Holmes seized a copy, casually indicating to the lad that I would pay him—a habit of his

I have always found particularly irritating—I managed to take in what he had been shouting at the passing crowds.

HORRIBLE MURDER ON THE MOORS! FAMOUS DETECTIVE KILLED!

Since it was perfectly obvious that Holmes had no intention of surrendering his copy, I instantly purchased another from the rather confused urchin whose confusion soon disappeared when I handed over a shilling and told him to keep the change.

The first few lurid paragraphs told the essence of the story . . .

"The blood-stained bodies of two men were found early this morning in a lonely part of the mist-shrouded Yorkshire moors . . ."

"Why," I thought, in this dreadful journalese, "are moors invariably 'mist-shrouded' and bodies 'blood-stained'?" Then I read on . . .

"Our local correspondent was fortunate enough to arrive at the scene with the local police, who were accompanied by Inspector Lestrade of Scotland Yard, who happened to be visiting the area . . ."

"Aha, Lestrade strikes again!" I must have said this aloud, for Holmes looked up from his paper and gave me a quizzical smile.

"Yes, it is indeed good to know that the long arm of Lestrade can reach so far. We can all sleep more easily in our beds for that knowledge." Then he buried himself again in the newsprint.

"In an exclusive interview with this paper Inspector Lestrade described the gruesome crime scene.

'On top of the ridge was the body of Harry Brotherton, a man who lived locally and was believed to have been an engineer by profession. He appeared to have been attacked by a large black dog. The dog's corpse was lying nearby and it had apparently been shot but not before it had mortally wounded Brotherton.

At the base of the cliff lay the body of another man, we have provisionally identified as Mr. Sherlock Holmes, the world famous consulting detective. I say "provisionally," although as someone who was a close personal friend of the deceased, I can really be in no doubt. On certain occasions in the past Mr. Holmes had been able to provide us with some small assistance in certain of our enquiries . . .' "

166

At that point I must have snorted in indignation, for Holmes looked up and remarked—

" 'Some small assistance'? I fancy Lestrade himself will blush when he reads it."

"You mean . . . ?"

"Lestrade never uttered a word, as far as I am aware. No, the account was fabricated by Mycroft and myself after you and Lestrade had retired last night. Mycroft sent it off in the early hours and since the Editor is a personal friend of his . . . Do you know, Watson, I do believe I could quite enjoy being a journalist for a while. It offers such a perfect opportunity to create the world as you would like it."

The rest of the story was in similar vein. Speculation that Holmes had been walking on the moor and come upon Brotherton just as the dog attacked. Holmes had clearly shot the beast, since a pistol was found near the detective's body. Then, rushing to help the injured Brotherton, he had slipped and fallen over the edge. These, it was emphasised, were preliminary findings prior to the local Coroner's autopsy report. Etc., etc.

Holmes waited for me to finish reading, then flourished his folded newspaper. "A *most* impeccable source, wouldn't you say, Watson?"

To which I could only answer by shaking my head in wonder.

CHAPTER FOURTEEN

I have always found the Café Royal a little florid for my taste. Perched a discreet but convenient distance from Piccadilly Circus, it conjures up images of assignations and intrigue. Hansom cabs debouching mysterious cloaked men and heavily-veiled women. And, of course, a more recent *habitué*, one Oscar Wilde, had only added to its air of glamorous notoriety.

It was with mixed feelings, then, but something of a *frisson* that I made my way through a convenient side door of that establishment as the clocks were striking a quarter to the hour of three that afternoon.

A discreet and neatly uniformed attendant was waiting to meet me and escort me to my *rendez-vous*. Not a word passed between us and once he had ushered me into a small cubicle of a room, he departed so silently that I might almost have imagined him.

It was then that I truly understood the cleverness of Holmes's choice of venue. This part of the establishment was devoted to private dining rooms—*salons privés*. To allow the management to accommodate different sizes of party, some of the rooms had been so arranged that a false wall could be moved back and forth to enlarge or reduce the size of the room at will. So artfully had this work of adaptation been carried out that, unless one knew the trick, it was virtually impossible to see what had been done.

I reflected on how many "private" conversations had, in fact, been rather less private than the participants had been led to believe. I hoped that this was about to be one of them.

Pulling up a small gilt chair as close to the dividing wall as I comfortably could, I settled down to wait for my "guests."

On the dot of three, I heard the door to the next room open. German punctuality I might have expected. Now for the true test. As they began to talk, I had to be careful not to let out an audible sigh of relief. The voices were muted but I could hear every word.

Someone spoke first over a rustle of paper.

"You've seen this, no doubt?"

The clipped, almost too perfect English of von Bork answered him.

"Naturally. My people brought it to me immediately. But it is not according to the plan we agreed. How did that meddling fool, Holmes get there? Brotherton was supposed to die alone, like the others. Geier was to let himself be seen as Holmes and then disappear—just like before. Someone has blundered!"

"Oh, come, come, Bork . . ." I noticed that the "von" was deliberately ignored and did I detect a slightly patronising edge to McDoum's voice? "Did you really expect to carry out this whole . . ." I felt he was on the verge of saying "charade" but instead he settled for "escapade"—"without Holmes picking up the trail at some point. The man's very cleverness was surely the whole reason that you wished to delete him from your equation? Let me tell you, my friend, it is as well for you that he is famous for working alone or you would have genuine cause to worry about whom he might have confided in . . ."

"You say he works alone. But what of his doctor friend—Wilson?"

"Watson. Nothing to worry about there. The man is a mere cypher, who exists merely to flatter Holmes's vanity. In any case, we have had him carefully watched since the affair began. We lost sight of him yesterday for a while but it is of no consequence. It is over. Game, set and match."

Von Bork interrupted him, the voice like liquid ice.

"It may be that my command of English is not as great as I had previously believed, my dear James, but I seem to hear your repeated use of the word 'you' and 'your,' when I would have thought 'our' was a more appropriate descriptor. Have you ceased to be involved in this little project of *ours?* Do I not seem to remember your insisting that, when the Great Day came—as come it will—you had the ambition to be made the Gauleiter for the province presently known as Scotland? The title of 'King,' I believe, though meaningless, would cause too many precedents in our subsequent 'acquisitions.' "

"Your memory is as meticulous as everything else about you," McDoum answered and then seemed to be thinking aloud . . .

The Thane of Cawdor lives,
A worthy gentleman . . .

"Ah, you British . . ."—this from von Bork—"always quoting Shakespeare. *Macbeth*, if I am not mistaken?"

McDoum's response was surprising. The man was clearly upset. "Never use the name! Call it 'the Scottish play'—if you must refer to it. To call it by name is to bring bad luck."

There was a moment's silence, then McDoum said in a more normal tone. "I apologise. I am over-reacting but old superstitions die hard and the last few weeks have . . ."

"Of course, my dear chap," von Bork interposed smoothly, like the career diplomat he was. "I quite understand. I confess I find myself a little tense from time to time as we near our goal. When one has the making of history in one's hands, a degree of stress is surely permissible?"

"You really believe that you—that *we*—can pull this off. The whole idea still beggars belief, that such a thing can happen so suddenly after centuries of world dominance. The British sun was never supposed to set and yet it goes out like a flickering candle in the first gust of wind?"

"Hardly a gust of wind, my dear McDoum. A silent and irresistible tempest would be a closer analogy. You are looking at the absolute moral and mental corruption created by nearly-absolute power. Success made the British soft. Luxury led to lethargy. The British see what they *want* to see. They do not want to see the rise of German might or, indeed the emergence of Japan—whose true voice the world has yet to hear. Ah, Germany and Japan—what a prospect! Rome and Greece co-existing . . .

"You see, my friend, your countrymen have forgotten what they once knew. They no longer fear the foreign devil—instead, they patronise him, make jokes about him. Maybe they invite him to their dinner parties and shooting week-ends to show him how civilised life should be lived. After all, anyone who saw the British way of life was bound to see the error of his pagan ways and grovel accordingly, and didn't all these foreign 'chiefs' send their children to English schools? If that didn't guarantee world peace— what did?"

Von Bork collected himself with an effort. "But I fear my enthusiasm is inclined to carry me away. To answer your question . . . the plan cannot possibly fail." There was messianic tone in the German's voice now. He was declaiming from his personal litany. "Everything has been calculated with psychological exactitude. The British are a weak, lazy people who believe what they wish to believe. They are fond of claiming that 'Britons never, never, never shall be slaves' and yet they were overrun by the Romans, the Danes, the Normans—a fact that they conveniently forget. Look at the Welsh, where the Spanish tiptoed in by the back door. No, they are a mongrel race, puffed up with false conceit. And what will make the whole thing ludicrously simple is that they hate each other as much as they hate—how do you say?—Johnny Foreigner . . .

"No, my friend, the quiet life is their ambition and we shall give them precisely that—on our terms, of course. There is only one element in any society that will cause the 'victim' to rebel against the 'victor' and fight to the last drop of his blood and that is a difference of religion. That is why you Protestant British have such trouble in Catholic Ireland and I would venture to suggest that it will go on being a problem—except that it will, of course, no longer be *your* problem."

"There's one other thing you may have under-estimated," McDoum replied, almost wistfully, I thought.

"And that is?"

"The young. They are the natural rebels and

what you propose will provide them with the perfect excuse to take up their arms."

"We have naturally factored that into our plans," von Bork said smugly. "In fact, we are counting on it. Far from confronting this younger generation, we shall gracefully capitulate to it. This is their country. We are merely good neighbours temporarily keeping a friendly eye on things for them. We shall invite them to take over government from their tired, discredited elders. We shall, of course, act as Regent for a brief period. Unfortunately, they will find the process fraught with infinitely more difficulty than they had imagined in their idealistic fervour. And then—as is the invariable way with the young— they will grow bored. They will be happy to turn the reins over to us as they look for their next source of instant gratification. A simple little plan, is it not? They will determine their own fate because of who and what they are.

"*Their* children, of course, will have no memory of the way it was. It is the birthright of the young to kick against the old ways—the *ancien regime*—if I may borrow from your old enemy. They will be part of the inventing of the New Britain—the 'Peoples' Britain.' Pardon me—I almost said the *Volksbritannia*. But that is, perhaps a *little* premature . . ."

McDoum made one more halfhearted try but I could tell from the sound of his voice that he knew the answer before he had finished the question.

"Yes, but supposing there *is* nationwide resistance to this—let's put no finer point upon it—this *occupation?*"

"Then our task becomes even simpler. We shall—how do you say?—'take off the gloves.' Once we have control of the seas, we shall patrol the English Channel and blockade you. An island—people will starve within a matter of days. This particular defeat would not be imperceptible—it would be ignominious."

As the man spoke, I felt my heart sink within me. Loath as I was to believe it, there was that in his argument that had the ring of bitter truth about it. How often had I complained to Holmes, to my cronies at the club, to practically anyone who would listen about the shortcomings of the youth of today? Of course, there was good in them—a great deal of it. Weren't many of them laying down their lives on the godforsaken African *veldt* at this very moment for a much more dubious cause than this? No, when the cause was clear, there was no doubt in my mind of the outcome. But yet there was this hedonistic streak that seemed to me daily more evident in the whole of our society and perhaps this was the crack that could destroy the whole edifice?

I became conscious of von Bork—or so I

assumed by the precision of the footsteps—pacing the room.

"Three and a quarter. And yet the man was so precise as to the time we should meet. Where is he?"

I could have told them that the missing fifteen minutes had been allowed precisely so that I might overhear a conversation such as the one they had just had. On the very dot of the quarter hour, there was a tap on the door and I heard—

"Gentlemen, a thousand pardons but I considered it wise to take a roundabout way to arrive here. One cannot be too careful, even though—ah, yes, I see you have read the news?"

I realised that I had never heard Geier's voice before. Nor, I suspect, had many people. The man let his face speak for him. I could only assume—knowing Holmes's thoroughness—that he had made it his business to do so. The English was slightly less perfect than von Bork's—a nicely deferential touch—but had a distinctly Germanic emphasis.

From the greeting both men seemed to be accepting him at face value.

"Congratulations," said McDoum, "a tidy job tidily done, especially considering . . ."

"But Holmes," von Bork interrupted, "how did *Holmes* get there?"

"Not entirely surprising, Baron," Geier responded. "Three of the four designers were killed. What other conclusion could anyone draw—let alone a man who prides himself on his deductive abilities—than the fact that the *fourth* man was inevitably at risk? Holmes would fly to him like a—homing pigeon? That's right, a homing pigeon. Sooner or later—and almost certainly sooner—the mysterious killer would strike again. To find his opponent and clear his name Holmes had no option but to be on the spot. Little did he realise that the essence of our plot was not the death of the four men but his own entanglement. As the English are fond of saying, he could not see the trees for the wood."

"The wood for the trees," McDoum corrected him.

"Exactly so. Thank you. The English idiom seems to follow no known laws of grammar. But I expect you gentlemen will soon correct such lack of order?"

"So Holmes is dead. You are sure of that?" von Bork insisted.

"I saw him with my own eyes," Geier responded. "The man who was Sherlock Holmes is taken care of."

"What happened precisely?"

"The dog was wrestling with Brotherton, as planned. Then Holmes appeared out of the mist and shot the animal. Brotherton was on the ground, too busy gasping for breath to see what happened next. I had been waiting close by and rushed up to Holmes. We struggled briefly on the edge—very much as he must have struggled with Moriarty at Reichenbach . . ."

Was it my imagination or did I hear a sudden intake of breath from one of the other two?

"And then . . ."

"And *then?*"

"And then there was only one Sherlock Holmes standing on the ledge. And he was soon swallowed up in the fog. Curtain. Applause."

"And you were not seen?"

"I passed myself off at the local inn, where the management will now swear that I was Holmes using an alias for some reason best known to himself. In the room I left various personal belongings that will verify that fact. The person who caught this morning's London train was someone else entirely. Do not concern yourselves, gentlemen. I bring you the package duly wrapped."

There was a pause and then Geier asked—"You have further instructions for me? You have need of my services for your meeting at Castle Doum?"

Even through the partition wall I could feel the silence as a physical presence.

When von Bork spoke the words were carved from ice.

"Where did you learn of such a meeting?"

"I eavesdropped outside the window of the

inn and heard Mycroft Holmes tell that stupid Inspector from Scotland Yard. It is interesting how much you can learn from listening in secret."

The answer seemed to satisfy von Bork, for he muttered to McDoum—"Yes, of course, he has the Prime Minister's ear—the Queen's, too, for that matter. He would know."

"The question is—how much *more* does he know?" There was evident concern in McDoum's voice. "We must accelerate our time table. And you know what the end of the month brings?"

Von Bork quickly cut him off. "Indeed, but we need not bother friend Geier with that. No, Herr Geier, I doubt that we shall be requiring your—unique—services again in this matter but I would, nonetheless, be grateful if you would hold yourself in readiness, just in case."

"Well, you know where to find me, gentlemen. Ah, many thanks . . ." It was obvious that something had been passed from hand to hand. "It is a pleasure to do business with you. Oh, there was one other thing—I nearly forgot. Naturally, I searched Holmes's body. The only thing of interest I found was this piece of paper . . ."

There was a moment's silence as the two men studied whatever Holmes had given them, then McDoum said in strangled tones . . .

"My God—it's the Dancing Men!"

"The *what?*"

"The Dancing Men. It was a cipher used in one of Holmes's recent cases. Don't you remember it from the notes Geier brought us? It happened a couple of years ago and led to several deaths. Holmes is threatening us from beyond the grave!"

"But what does it *say,* man? You're the one who gave us the ideas for the other murders, because you said you had personal reasons to remember every one of Holmes's cases that Watson fellow had ever published. So *read* it!"

"I can't. Only Holmes ever truly deciphered it!"

In the ensuing silence I heard Holmes/Geier say—"In that case perhaps I should have brought Mr. Holmes back with me. As it is, I'm afraid this is beyond my own small talents, so I will bid you *auf wiedersehen,* gentlemen. By the way, I notice that there are sixty-four of the little fellows, if that means anything . . ."

There was a sharp clicking of heels and a moment later I heard the door of the next room close softly.

I sat perfectly still until my neighbours had left. So many things now made a disturbing kind of sense but one small question flitted around in my mind like a butterfly that refuses to settle.

Why had von Bork called McDoum "my dear James"—when his name was Angus?

• • •

I arrived back in Baker Street to find the sitting room in darkness, even though it was barely five o'clock. I could not understand why Mrs. Hudson should have drawn the curtains so early, when the autumn light was only just beginning to fade.

Then I heard Holmes's voice from his chair.

"Oblige me by only turning on that table light, would you, Watson?"

I did as he requested and looked at the man sitting opposite me. He was Holmes and yet not Holmes. He had not tried to do anything to disguise his height and general build yet there was something different about the face. Somehow he had managed to give it that bland, plastic quality that was Geier's—a human canvas waiting for the artist.

"I'm afraid I must once more make myself scarce, old fellow. It would never do for our friends to see Sherlock Holmes pottering around London when he is supposed to be deceased and defunct. A few more days and the crisis will have passed—one way or another."

"Is that what they meant by their time table?" I asked.

"Indeed. The Navy's lease on the harbour runs out at the end of the month—on October 2nd, to be precise—by which time *The Phantom*'s sea trials will be over. I think it hardly coincidence that the event planned at Castle Doum takes place on the day immediately preceding. Whatever is to happen will assuredly link those two locations and be planned to create the most newsworthy event they can contrive. We shall, of course, see to it that they do not succeed."

I was about to say that this could prove difficult, since we did not know what their intention was but I refrained. Holmes would tell me in his own good time and hand me my part. I should know soon enough whether I was to play a leading part or merely carry a spear.

He made a move in his chair preparatory to rising but I was not about to let him go quite so easily.

"The Dancing Men?"

"Ah, yes, the Dancing Men. I suspect that they will, indeed lead our friends a merry dance—perhaps even The Dance of Death. You will remember, old fellow, that I have made a modest study of all forms of secret writings and have even penned a trifling monograph upon the subject?"

"Naturally. You analysed one hundred and sixty separate ciphers, if I'm not mistaken. I have it filed over there."

Holmes picked up a piece of paper from the table beside him and passed it across to me. I unfolded it and saw the familiar capering figures of the matchstick men, drawn in a childlike hand. Their antics seemed to mock the reader. . . . The opening lines looked as follows . . .

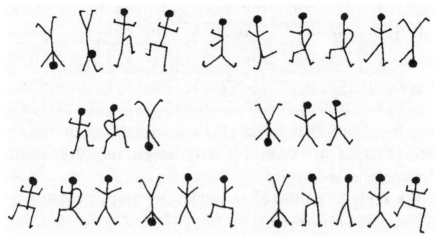

"And yet those cheerful little fellows eluded me far too long, because I insisted on complicating matters unnecessarily. I should have remembered my own maxim that simplicity is the key to complexity. I *saw* them but I did not observe."

"But what makes you think the Germans will not crack the code eventually?"

"Oh, they will—eventually—but their convoluted turn of mind will frustrate them for the longest time and when they finally do unlock the message, it will mean worse than nothing to them."

"Nothing?"

"Watson, I hardly think that a quotation from Mr. Lewis Carroll's *Jabberwocky* will aid them in their plan for world domination.

Twas brillig and the slithy toves
Did gyre and gimble in the wabe,
All mimsy were . . .

And the fact that the message is a letter short of the supposed sixty-four will exercise them greatly. Does a comma count as a letter? How many angels can dance on the head of a pin? A race without a sense of humour—or at least irony—does not deserve to dominate anyone or anything. And now I really must make myself literally scarce."

As he moved towards his room, I could restrain myself no longer.

"The final round, eh, Holmes?"

"Yes, but not the beginning of the end, old friend. I prefer to think of it as 'the end of the beginning.' I say, that sounds quite good, doesn't it? You might care to jot it down, Watson, before I forget it. Or someone else uses it first."

He left the room but a moment later the door opened and a hand tossed a bulky envelope at my feet. A diminishing voice said—

"Your marching orders, my dear fellow. Oh, and you might take your friend, Mr. Eley for company. *Such* a persuasive fellow . . ."

CHAPTER FIFTEEN

Major Abernetty? Major *Abernetty?*"
I turned to see who was being paged. And then I remembered—*I* was Major Abernetty, Major Charles Abernetty (Retired), Special Correspondent of *The Times*, here in Invercrory to attend the Special Summit meeting at Castle Doum the following day.

Holmes's instructions had been highly specific. Mycroft had pulled a number of strings with the Editor of "The Thunderer." Abernetty was supposedly a man of about my own age and general appearance and a recent appointee, who would thus be unknown to his brother scribes. His "record" now safely filed in the paper's archives, was reassuringly detailed and entirely fictitious. Hopefully, I would satisfy the prying eyes that would inevitably seek it out, once my participation was announced.

Over the years I had learned enough from Holmes to have mastered the rudiments of disguise and to following his dictum of less being more.

A small amount of putty to enlarge the nose, a spot of dye to give my moustache more of a salt and pepper look, a pair of heavy tortoise-shell glasses and a balding hairpiece wrought significant changes to my normal appearance. The wig was the only thing I really objected to, since I am quite proud to have maintained a good head of hair so relatively late in life. My friends at the club would not have recognised me when I had finished my transformation, nor would I have wished them to do so. Was this—I thought, as I inspected my handiwork in the Baker Street mirror before leaving for the station—the shape of things to come?

So here I was, one of a dozen or so journalists from the world's leading newspapers, waiting in this out-of-season Scottish seaside hotel to be ferried to Castle Doum at first light to report on the historic Summit meeting. At the end of his letter Holmes had appended the postscript—"See and observe. Omit no detail, however trifling. As for me, my dear fellow, do not worry if you do not see me. But—like the poor—I shall always be with you!"

Already I had met several of my "colleagues." There was Soper from the *Chronicle*, complaining as a matter of habit that anything that was about to transpire—whatever it might be— was undoubtedly a plot to undermine the working man. There were representatives of various European journals, all of whom seemed pro- grammed to behave according to their national stereotypes, most particularly the German, Zuberbier, who seemed determined to assert a moral supremacy before the meeting had even started. "There were much ground rules to be established," he assured everyone who would listen, "was it not so? We must all play the straight wicket." The fact that no one else seemed prepared to even debate the point apparently bothered him not at all.

We had been scheduled to "meet our Doum"— as Soper insisted on putting it with monotonous regularity—that evening, except for the late arrival of the French and American contingent. I saw from the list that our numbers would be completed by the addition of Monsieur Aristide Nemo of the Paris Press Bureau and Quentin E. Dowd of *The New York Times* and in my mind's eye I could just visualise both of them. Or were recent events making me more than usually xenophobic?

Finally the landlord's repeated call broke through my reverie.

"Major Abernetty?"

"Yes, yes—sorry, I was miles away," I apologised as I approached the bar. "What can I do for you?"

"Not for me, Major. For the young man sitting on his own at the corner table. He's anxious to meet you and asked me to point you out."

I looked down to the end of the bar. The holiday season, such as it might be in this wind-swept northern retreat, was most definitely a thing of the past and we journalists were the hotel's only guests. A relentlessly rainy evening had driven everyone to the comparative companionability of the bar, where they were now standing around in small, culturally-aligned groups taking their pleasures all too seriously. Something in the dour Scots mist seemed to have permeated them, even the normally ebullient Soper. Doum apparently spelled gloom.

The only obvious exception seemed to be the solitary young man sitting alone with a tankard of the local beer in front of him. He was slender and somewhere in his early twenties. A cowlick of dark hair flopped over his forehead and the eyes were bright as he looked up at me when I approached him. I was pleased to see that he rose in deference to an older man.

Sticking out a hand, he pumped mine effusively.

"Good to see you again, Major," he said.

"Er—good to see you, too," I replied.

"And how's your good lady? Muriel, isn't it?"

"Oh, splendid, splendid. Never been better." I had been fearful that something like this would happen.

"And the boys?"

"Ah, well, you know boys . . . ?"

"Indeed I do," the young man replied, indicating the empty seat next to him, which I had little alternative but to take. Then he dropped his voice. "But I also happen to know that the real

Major Abernetty is a widower and childless. I seem to have studied your résumé better than you have. No, don't worry, Doctor Watson . . ."

I had half risen but he pulled me back into my seat.

"I can only deduce that after your partner's tragic death, you are here to complete some unfinished business. In which case, as someone who has read with total admiration every word you have published, I would consider it the greatest possible honour if you would consider me your 'Watson' while you carry it out, for I know it cannot be a trivial matter."

He stuck out that enthusiastic hand again and pumped mine, if anything, even more effusively.

"My name's Buchan—John Buchan."

Words rarely fail me but on this occasion they did. Then instinct took over. What were my choices? Bluff would get me nowhere with a young man as sharp as this one. And there was something about him that I liked. Would I have done the same at his age? I'd like to think that I might.

By and large, I think I've been a pretty good judge of men. I made my mind up there and then. May Holmes forgive me if I'm wrong.

"Not another Watson, I think. How about a first Buchan?"

And we shook hands for the third time.

Over the next hour—with the wind whistling

outside like a dervish and rattling the windows as though to shake us all loose for being there out of season—I learned more about this unusual young man.

"I want to be a writer, too—Major. I've had one thing published so far . . . a sort of historical story called *John Burnet of Barns*. It hasn't done badly but it's not what I *really* want to write. I want to try something more exciting, adventure stuff—more like yours. It's the *way* you tell those tales, Doctor—Major—that brings them right off the page."

I thought of the number of times Holmes had looked down that aquiline nose of his at what he considered my "embellishments" and wished that he were here now to hear my "public" giving its verdict. It also occurred to me to wonder whether Holmes's own perception would be modified if I were to give him a share of the royalties but it was an unworthy thought and I pushed it to the back of my mind.

Buchan was speaking again.

"Don't tell me more than you feel able but there's some pretty big game afoot, isn't there, sir?" For some reason I liked the "sir." "All this Anglo-German business, kissing cousins, brothers under the skin, just doesn't ring true to me. That's why I got the local paper to sign me up as their representative for this trip. The people at SAGS weren't keen at all but for some reason they don't want to make a fuss in the community, so I'm in. But in *what*—that's what I'd like to know?"

I told him as much as I felt I could without betraying any confidences. There were those of us who felt that something destructive to our country's good was being planned here to coincide with this meeting and, whatever it turned out to be, we intended to do our level best to stop it.

The bright eyes blazed even brighter and the cowlick dipped further over one eye in his excitement. He was positively enjoying the prospect, which, I had to confess to myself, was more than I was. Where—oh, where—was Holmes?

"We Scots must stick together," said Buchan effusively. "Doctor, I'm your man!" And, if I hadn't happened to pick up my glass at that moment, he would have shaken my hand again.

Then I became aware of a change in the noise level in the bar. A door was opened, letting in a draught of cold air and rain and when it closed two men were standing in the room, shaking the water from their clothes.

Both were tall and thin but there the resemblance ended. The one who introduced himself primly as Aristide Nemo wore a flamboyant white suit with a red silk cravat and—I shuddered slightly at the sight—a matching red handkerchief tucked in the sleeve of his jacket! His hair looked as though it were made of black patent leather and he sported a small, perfectly-manicured goatee beard. A pair of rimless *pince-nez* adorned his long, thin nose. My abiding impression was that he appeared poorly equipped to face our harsh northern clime.

He insisted on shaking hands with each and every one of us, bowing over the clasped hands and murmuring *"Enchanté"* without any great show of conviction. Young Buchan looked positively apprehensive, as though he half expected Nemo to kiss his hand.

In marked contrast, his companion presented a distinctly formal appearance. Neatly suited and ramrod straight, with his short hair and sober tie, Quentin E. Dowd of *The New York Times* was the very image of the educated East Coast Yankee. The voice had that Bostonian nasal twang that distorts certain words for English ears but the manners were every bit as meticulous as Nemo's.

The contrast extended to the manner of greeting. Whereas Nemo's was perfunctory, Dowd made eye contact as he took your hand firmly in both of his and he had the American knack—which I have always envied—of knowing the names (both Christian and surnames) of everyone in the room. By the time he had completed his tour of inspection, we all seemed to be old friends at some class reunion.

He seemed to pay particular attention to our table.

"You're that Buchan fellow, eh? Enjoyed that first book of yours. Lookin' forward to many more. Guess one day we'll all find ourselves characters in one of 'em. What do you say, Major?"

I nodded feebly. Right now that was the least of my worries. The first was to locate Holmes. Unless he'd spirited himself into Castle Doum, it seemed almost certain that he was in this very room under my own eyes. But whose identity had he taken?

Zuberbier, the caricature German *junker*? Too obvious, surely? The garrulous Soper? Possible. Holmes fancied himself as a member of the proletariat. I scanned the rest of the party but saw nothing to arrest my attention. But then, *nothing* was precisely what Holmes always boasted a man would see when he chose to make himself undetectable.

I came back to the two latest arrivals and immediately my mind was made up. It had to be the Frenchman. The sheer *bravura* of the role was what would appeal to the actor in him. Looking back on recent events, it suddenly came to me in a blinding flash that the entire episode with The Great Mysterioso had disturbed Holmes in more ways than one. For once in his life he had been literally upstaged. Now it was his turn. Yes,

Nemo was *definitely* the one. And of course—why hadn't I thought of it before?—"Nemo" meant "no one." A man who didn't exist—because he was Sherlock Holmes!

I was so pleased with my deduction I would dearly have liked to share it with him. In fact, so taken was I that I almost missed the landlord's announcement that the boat for the Isle of Doum would be leaving from the jetty at eight a.m. sharp and calling for last orders.

At which point Zuberbier climbed heavily on to a small table that creaked under his weight and called for a toast.

"Well, fellows, here we are having the good time, isn't it? I am proposing a toast to the perennial comradeship and fine feelings spreading."

There were a few cynical smiles at the overtness of the sentiment—as well as the awkwardness of the expression—but one by one everyone raised his glass and murmured a subdued toast.

And then I heard Dowd say clearly—"Today England. Tomorrow—the US of A? Then—why not the world, eh?"

Zuberbier looked at him keenly and for a moment the clown's face was gone.

"Why not, indeed?" Then he was down from the table, back in the group slapping every back in reach.

Buchan turned to me and I could see that he shared my revulsion for the sentiment.

"If you'll excuse me—er, Major—I think I'll turn in before he dislocates my vertebrae. And don't forget—I'm your man. And maybe Mr. Dowd is right—maybe there *will* be a book in it." And with that he reached across and almost dislocated my wrist with a final handshake.

The morning mist parted like a theatre curtain and the Isle of Doum was suddenly louring over us.

"Positively Wagnerian," said a voice behind me. I turned to find Dowd at my elbow. "Reminds me of *Siegfried* at the Met."

And indeed it was an austerely impressive sight. The cliffs rose sheer in all directions that we could see and the sea birds wheeling around the summit, crying like lost souls warning us to stay away or share their fate, merely added to the theatricality of the scene. It was as though some primeval god had pushed his thumb up from the centre of the earth and ejected this random plug of rock, then proceeded to forget about it. Although the island was a scant half mile from the mainland, it seemed like a lost world of its own.

Dowd must have read my thoughts, for he said—"I'm told the aspect is rather more pleasing from the other side, Major."

A few moments later his prophecy was fulfilled, as the fishing smack that had brought us

195

from Invercrory—some of us in more apparent comfort than others—rounded a headland there was Castle Doum straight ahead of us.

A quotation surfaced in my own mind. It was from a school production of *Richard III*—

> And all the clouds that lour'd upon our
>   house
> In the deep bosom of the ocean buried

—and it now made sense to me for the first time.

It was truly an impressive sight. Solidly built of granite, it stood with four square Scots rectitude gazing out across the North sea, as if daring any intruder to even consider making the trip. The cliffs were still steep but I could see a path snaking its way up from a small jetty on which a landing party of black clad men were standing to attention in expectation of our arrival.

To the right of the main island I could just make out what looked like a small appendage of rock that almost resembled a tail and what looked like a set of rough hewn steps leading down to it . . .

. . . and then I was distracted by a French-accented voice.

"From Wagner to Tennyson, surely?

> Four grey walls and four grey towers,
> Overlook a space of flowers . . .

Of course, I cannot guarantee flowers at this time of the year and I very much doubt if we shall find the Lady of Shalott in residence, but the sentiment is a good one, no?"

I turned to find Nemo standing next to Dowd. Did these two hunt in a pack? He seemed to ignore my scrutiny and fixed his gaze on the reception committee, thoughtfully stroking his small beard.

Holmes—I thought to myself—these little gestures will be the undoing of you. I made a note to myself to slip it into the conversation one evening in Baker Street when he was being more than usually pleased with something he had done.

"You're smiling, Major?" It was young Buchan now who had joined our little group. "You must have seen something I've missed. What *are* we doing on this benighted chunk of rock?"

There was a soft thump as the fishing boat nosed into the jetty and was secured by several unsmiling attendants. As we were gathering our belongings, Zuberbier bustled self-importantly forward and was deferentially helped to step ashore.

It was then that I realised he had been sent to monitor us while we were on the mainland. Our friends were taking no chances and I felt the small knot of anxiety in my stomach take another turn. Perhaps I had been inclined to take these people too lightly. There was clearly a formidable organisation at work, considering how quickly they had had to move to organise this event.

"Attention, fellows, if you please!" Zuberbier was addressing us, as though we were new recruits in his platoon. "You will now be taken to your accommodations and one of these excellent gentlemen . . ." he indicated the group of distinctly unsmiling men standing behind him with their arms folded—"will be at your personal disposal for the length of your stay here." Then he added as an after-thought and concession. "Which we hope will be a constructive one. And now, if I may make an English joke—Let us go and meet our doum!"

"Anglo-German solidarity? I think not, monsieur," Nemo whispered in my ear. "If they can show a British passport between them, then my name is not Aristide Nemo . . ."

"Aha, but it's *not,*" I very nearly said.

The rest of the day was something of an anti-climax. After being shown to our individual rooms—somewhat monastic though perfectly comfortable—we were taken on a guided tour of the "grounds" by Zuberbier, who had appointed himself—or, more likely, been appointed—our tour guide.

The "space of flowers" turned out to be a walled garden in which a few hardy bushes were putting up a losing fight with the bleakness of the northern elements. Beyond it was a short paved walkway ending in a chain-link fence beyond which a path could be discerned, presumably leading down to the shore line. In the middle of the fence was a metal gate, firmly locked and chained.

"Where's the key for when I take me constitutional?" asked Soper, more, it seemed, to be provocative than as a serious request.

"Unfortunately, that will not be possible, Herr Soper," Zuberbier answered smoothly. "The cliffs are—how you say?—'brittle' here. Most unsafe. There have been many accidents and, as our special guests, your safety is our obligation."

"But obviously not our pleasure," Buchan muttered at my side. "And what's all this 'our' stuff? No mention of McDoum since we've been here. Doesn't *he* own this place?"

And indeed we had yet to lay eyes on either of our nominal hosts. To all intents and purposes we were paying guests in some German *schloss*.

As we were shepherded back to the Castle, I thought I saw Soper eyeing the gate thoughtfully.

For the rest of the day we might as well have gone back to school. We were gathered into the Library, which had been converted into a kind of lecture hall with an improvised dais at one end. Seated on the platform looking down at us were several impassive men who proceeded to deliver a series of highly detailed lectures on various aspects of German history and culture. A few of them had made clumsy attempts to adapt their material to the present theme of Anglo-German relations but it was apparent that what we were receiving was a *blitzkrieg* of well-prepared propaganda.

Once again it was Buchan who expressed my own uneasy thoughts.

"How long have these laddies been putting this stuff together, I wonder?"

To which Dowd from my other side murmured, as the last lecturer put down his notes—"I believe we now know more about the Hohenzollerns than we reasonably *wanted* to know. Ah, here comes our Master of Ceremonies . . ."

The indefatigable Zuberbier was on his feet again with the air of a cat that has just eaten everyone else's share of the cream. Turning to the lecturers, he thanked them fulsomely for their "inspiring insightfulness" and led a ragged round of applause in which we joined reluctantly.

"And now, my good old fellows," he said, turning to us, "we have had the inspirations. We have earned the recreations, *ja*? Tonight we are the honoured guests of Sir Angus McDoum and the Graf von Bork. You will have the good time." With that instruction to rejoice we were virtually shooed from the room.

I turned to say something to Buchan but he was nowhere to be seen.

• • •

Dinner was, admittedly, a more congenial affair, if one by-passed some of the German delicacies on offer. Sauerkraut has never been one of my predilections and there seemed to be endless variants of it at every turn. I observed that many of my "colleagues" were experiencing the same qualms but we all managed to find something on the menu that served its purpose.

McDoum and von Bork were now amply in evidence and handled themselves well, finding the opportunity to talk to everyone individually. Clearly, they had both been well briefed and were able to demonstrate personal knowledge of each man's background. It is a tactic calculated to stroke the vanity of any guest and journalists are no less susceptible than anyone else. I won't say our hosts had them eating out of their hands but much of the earlier tension was being dispersed as the evening wore on and I could not help but wonder whether this, too, was not part of the overall plan.

When von Bork came over to me, I confess I felt a little apprehensive as my mind tried to recall the salient details of my new identity. After a few pleasantries von Bork's chill blue eyes met mine.

"Tell me, Major, where have we met before? Something about you is quite familiar."

"Oh," I said, as casually as I could manage,

"probably some army event. You're a military man yourself, I believe?"

"Very likely, very likely. One of those occasions where we all relive past glories and where *some* . . ." he clearly exempted himself from what was to come—"justify past defeats. Which of your own exploits do you hold in your heart, Major?" And again he held my eyes with his own.

"Oh, the Battle of Maiwand, without any doubt." Now I felt on safe ground once more.

"Really? I did not realise that you had served in India. I was under the impression . . ." And then I realised that the real Major Abernetty had served everywhere *but* India.

Before I could enmesh myself further, for my mental reflexes are not always of the quickest, I was saved by a voice at my side.

"You talk of battles? Was there ever such a travesty as—?" And Nemo mentioned an encounter in the Franco-Prussian War that immediately distracted von Bork completely, as Nemo must have known it would. As they were arguing, accompanied by staccato hand chops on von Bork's part and continuous shoulder shrugging on Nemo's, I beat a hasty retreat.

As I passed another small group, a hand reached out and tapped me on the shoulder.

"I'd give that one a wide berth, if I were you, Major," said Quentin E. Dowd, "unless you want another war wound."

I puzzled over his remark for the remainder of the evening. *I* certainly suffered from one—but did the Major?

Discretion being distinctly the better part of valour, I was one of the first of the group to retire for the night. To be honest, the strain of occupying someone else's persona was proving a strain and the intellectual battering we had received earlier in the day had left me with the desire to have as good a night's sleep as I was likely to manage in a strange bed. Tomorrow would be decisive in one way or another and I wanted time to organise my thoughts before then.

What exactly was Holmes expecting from me? Come to that, what was he expecting at all? Tomorrow night was to be the grand banquet to be graced by the presence of Prince Edward, the Prince of Wales, heir apparent to the British throne. It was to be—McDoum and von Bork had assured us earlier—a coming together of kindred spirits, an historic fusing of mighty forces, the superlative analogies were endless. And, they reminded us, our own presence showed that the whole world was indeed watching.

Yet how did this goodwill mission fit into the pattern of disruption that Mycroft and Holmes foresaw? There had to be something more that was not yet clear to me.

I was mulling all this over and must have fallen

asleep in my chair when there was a discreet tap at my door. As I shook myself awake I saw that the fire was reduced to embers. A glance at my watch showed me that it was now nearly two in the morning.

All of this must have taken me longer than I thought in my befuddled state, for an impatient voice close to the keyhole hissed—"It's only me, Doctor—Buchan. There's something I think you should see."

I unlocked the door and a moment later he was hovering excitedly in the doorway, urging me to follow him.

"We must be quiet. They are everywhere and there seem to be more of them than when we arrived. Something pretty rum is going on here but that's not the rummiest thing . . . ." And raising a finger to his lips to enjoin me to silence, he took my arm and led me along the corridor and up a spiral staircase I had not noticed earlier.

I realised that we were now high up in one of the "four grey towers" and overlooking the side of the island by which we had arrived. As I looked down from this precipitous height I could see the jetty. Despite the late hour, it was swarming with the mysterious men in black, all busily carrying large boxes up to the main house. They must have been wearing rubber or rope-soled shoes for not a sound carried on the night air and the silence made their activities all the more sinister.

But it was not the silent toilers that were exciting Buchan's interest. Even though there was no realistic chance of our being overheard at such a remove, it was in a whisper close to my ear that he spoke.

"I found this passage way soon after we arrived, Doctor. I imagine they thought they'd locked it but the catch hadn't quite caught and I was able to 'persuade' it to let me in. I've been keeping an eye on the comings and goings since everyone turned in and I tell you—there have been quieter evenings at Glasgow Central Station.

"It started with one of our chaps sneaking out—I think it was Soper. Then Zuberbier came out with one of the guards—because that's what they are, to put no finer point upon it. The guard was very excited and kept pointing the way Soper had gone. After a while Zuberbier took off in the same direction and no sooner had *he* gone than Nemo appears from behind that buttress and follows *him*—just like 'Follow My Leader.' At least, I'm pretty *sure* it was Nemo, although he, too, was dressed all in black. Soon after all this lot started . . ." and he indicated the worker ants down below us.

"I can't make head or tail of it, to tell you the truth, Doctor, but I can tell you I don't like it one bit. But that isn't what I wanted to show you. Look!" And he raised a hand and pointed out to sea.

At first I could see nothing but the matte black sky. A low cloud cover had obliterated the stars and it was like peering into a void. Then I saw a series of intermittent flashes of light—a mere pinpoint that came and went . . . came and went. Someone in a boat offshore was signalling to the castle.

And now the man in charge of the loading party had picked up a darkened lantern and was signalling back, raising and lowering a shutter in the same staccato fashion.

"Can you read Morse code, Doctor," Buchan hissed, "because I'm fairly sure that's what it is?"

"Curse it, no," I replied. "If only we had Holmes here. Codes are child's play to him. He'd decipher it in a moment."

"I think you'll find it says—SIEGFRIED SEHR GUT—which either means that someone on the island has a friend called Siegfried who is feeling in good health or—which I believe to be infinitely more probable—the German operation, code named 'Siegfried,' is primed and ready for action. Good evening, gentlemen. Watson, I really cannot believe this cold night air is good for your lumbago. We don't want you below par tomorrow . . ."

"Holmes!"

I turned to find myself staring at a smiling— Quentin E. Dowd.

206

・ ・ ・

"But you *can't* be Holmes. *Nemo* is Holmes . . ."

By the time I realised how foolish I sounded, Holmes was laughing that distinctive mirthless laugh of his. Buchan was standing with his mouth ajar, looking at us as though we were both mad.

"I mean—Nemo is 'no one.' " Even that didn't sound much better.

"As usual, old friend, you have sprayed the truth with grapeshot. There is certainly no one called 'Aristide Nemo' in the Paris Press Bureau but there *is* a man who uses that pseudonym— among others—in the Paris *Deuxième Bureau*, the Government department that deals with sensitive matters of national security and espionage. Our paths have crossed more than once in the past. Watson, you may remember the case of Huret, the Boulevard Assassin?"

I did—vividly. "So that was . . . ?"

"If you don't mind, I have promised to keep his real identity a secret. In his line of work it can mean the difference between life and death. Ironically, in his spare time—heaven knows where he finds it!—he acts as a consulting detective and has been kind enough to say that he uses as his model a certain practitioner in Baker Street. I have warned him that if he follows my example any more closely, he will end up as the hero of some cosy detective stories written by some middle-aged lady with literary pretensions in which he uses his limited English and his little grey cells to solve some exotic conundrum. What a fate!"

"Oh, come, Holmes, that's a little far-fetched."

"Possibly, possibly. And by the way, old fellow, if you're playing word games with names, why didn't it occur to you that you had another one right under your nose? 'Quentin E. Dowd . . . , Q.E.D.' Shame on you, Watson!"

"Talking of *names,* Holmes," I interrupted, anxious to divert the conversation from my own powers of deduction, "you landed me with Abernetty. Why did you choose that particular name?"

He gave me a quizzical look and answered— "Surely you remember that dreadful business of the Abernetty family? It was a circumstance I was only able to solve by my chance observation of the depth to which the parsley had sunk into the butter on a particularly hot day. Surmising that the circumstances in which you were likely to find yourself might verge on the heated, the name simply popped into my mind. I've no doubt our friend Freud could provide a more complex explanation but that is the best I can do, I fear."

Then in a trice the levity was gone and in its place a complete focus of his attention, as a soft but unmistakable footfall was heard on the stair.

A moment later Nemo was at our side. A glance at our faces told him all he needed to know. He acknowledged us with a quick pat on the arm and turned to Holmes.

"It is as we thought, my friend. The island is secured and they have men and *matériel* hidden in the cellars. I overheard Zuberbier talking to von Bork. Whatever they have planned will take place at 8 o'clock tomorrow night . . ."

"Which gives His Royal Highness ample time to walk into a neat little trap." Holmes was looking thoughtfully out to sea as he spoke.

"But we must get a message to him," I expostulated. "Somehow we must stop him coming."

"No, Watson, that is the one thing we must *not* do. Don't you see that it is imperative that we make them commit themselves, so that we can expose their true intentions? They must play their hand—and we must trump it. This time at least we know what they plan. Next time we may not."

He turned to Nemo. "What about Soper?"

"The man has the heart of a lion but the brains of a *mouche*! I followed him as close as I could along the cliffs and there I lost him. There was a gap forced in the perimeter fence and that must be his doing. The fool is determined to bring about—what do you say?—'scoop'? It is he who will be 'scooped,' I fear.

"Before he distracted me, I did as you asked and examined the shoreline. Since there are so many men moving about and I was dressed as they were, there was little chance of my being noticed. I observed signs of many boats landing on the beach . . ."

"Rehearsals, no doubt." Holmes spoke to himself.

"And I found this . . ."

He handed Holmes a metal badge of the sort one might pin on a jacket or shirt. Holmes held it up to the window of the tower where the moon had now decided to grace us with its fitful presence.

I could discern the design of a clenched fist grasping a letter 'A'.

"The Sons of Albion," Holmes murmured. "A Free Britain. But the badge, I see, was made in Germany. Most interesting."

Like a good actor who has delivered his big speech, Nemo gave us all a small bow from the waist.

"And now, if you gentlemen will excuse me, I shall return to my room, enjoy a quiet cognac and read until I fall asleep. I am particularly intrigued at the moment by a *roman* entitled 'The Musgrave Ritual.' Totally implausible, of course. You may know it, Doctor—I mean, Major."

A moment later both Nemo and Dowd had vanished as if they were figments of our imagination, leaving a subdued Buchan to help a bemused Abernetty retrace his steps to his room, where curiously enough, he proceeded to sleep like a child.

CHAPTER SIXTEEN

The news was announced next morning over the communal breakfast.

Zuberbier asked for a moment's silence. There had been an unfortunate accident. One of our dear colleagues, Herr Soper, had apparently been taking an "unauthorised walk" the previous evening. A section of the treacherous cliff face had given way, causing the unfortunate man to plunge to his death. In this time of grief he was sure we would be comforted to hear that the Society for Anglo-German Solidarity would be making a generous donation to the man's immediate family. In addition, SAGS would be setting up a Harold Soper Memorial bequest to fund journalists dedicated to this great cause for which their colleague had died.

He was sure that Herr Soper would not wish this unfortunate happening to distract us from the great work that would be completed this day. We would now all rise and pay our respects to our dear departed colleague and friend . . .

I caught Holmes's eye at the other end of the refectory table. So the gloves were now off?

Not surprisingly, the news cast a pall over the group. The sense of being prisoners rather than guests seemed to increase and the atmosphere at the morning's "briefing session" was positively funereal.

Von Bork spoke of "this historic moment" in the history of our two great peoples. McDoum added his conviction that we were embarking upon "a century of destiny." We all wrote dutifully in our notebooks but the usual jocular cynicism that characterises any gathering of journalists was totally absent from the gathering. Just before noon McDoum released us to refresh ourselves before the arrival of "our very special guest." We would foregather at seven o'clock sharp to be ready to greet him.

As the group dispersed, I found myself walking beside an impassive Dowd.

"What now, Holmes?" I said, giving a fair imitation—I thought—of a ventriloquist.

"This particular serpent has two heads—that we *know* of," he murmured. "When the crisis is reached, you and I will take on McDoum, while Nemo and Buchan will keep an eye on von Bork. Oh, don't worry, old fellow," he added, seeing my look of concern, "I have already briefed them. Nemo has been in many a tight corner and I fancy young Buchan can look after himself.

"And now—since I see we have a little time at our disposal, I shall go to my room and study the motets of Lassus. They concentrate the mind wonderfully."

And he walked away from me down the corridor as though he hadn't a care in the world.

I believe history will record that one of Queen Victoria's more lasting legacies was that of royal punctuality. Her son Edward's entourage arrived promptly as the castle's clocks were striking seven.

We were told that the fact of his already being in residence at Balmoral—the family's summer retreat—had made the royal presence possible. Preceded by McDoum and von Bork and surrounded by the black clad attendants, the royal party entered the main hall where we were all assembled and made their way to the dais.

I had never seen our future monarch in person before but, like everyone else in the room, I had seen his portrait countless times in the newspapers and magazines, so the man looked uncannily familiar.

Now a man of nearly sixty, he wore the signs of good living like a badge. Tall and heavy set, it was as though he had extracted his revenge for having been made to wait so long for his inheritance by indulging his body. But the eyes told one immediately that inhabiting that huge frame was a quick and clever inner man. The eyes missed nothing. As he settled himself in his chair, they were scanning the room face by face.

Was it my imagination but did they seem to linger on me longer than my allocated time?

Looking around in my own turn, I could see Dowd and Nemo strategically placed at opposite sides of the room with Buchan unobtrusively seated in the back row near the door. All we had to do now was wait—but for what?

The meeting began with the usual fawning greetings that any member of a reigning house must expect to contend with on a public occasion. How deeply grateful we all were . . . a man of such varied accomplishments . . . the deep family connections with Germany . . . von Bork and McDoum droned on in what was essentially a recapitulation of all that we had heard the previous day. When would they ever get to the point?

And then it struck me that this *was* the point. There was no other. These men were playing for time, filling the air with words until some prearranged moment was reached. A glance was enough to tell me that Holmes and Nemo had reached the identical conclusion. The clock was ticking toward the hour of eight.

Perhaps it was this heightened awareness that made me conscious of the fact that I was myself once again the object of unusual scrutiny. Freud could probably explain what it is in the human brain that makes one physically aware that another person is looking at you less than casually. All I knew was that someone was doing that to me at that very moment.

Since I was sitting in the front row, I had to affect to be making myself more comfortable in my seat, so that I could take in the rest of the room. No, all the other journalists were sitting in a variety of bored or uncomfortable postures. None of them.

Turning back, I realised that my observer was seated on the platform. It was none other than the Prince of Wales himself—and he was trying to catch my eye! In this he certainly succeeded. Then, as I returned his stare—very much, I imagine, as a rabbit is transfixed by a fox—the Prince's left eyelid distinctly drooped. In anyone else it would have qualified as a wink . . .

And then—even more disconcertingly—he raised a finger to his lips. To the rest of the room it must have looked like the familiar gesture of a man narcissistically stroking his moustache but I knew it for some kind of warning.

But before I could sort out the questions teeming through my brain, the great double doors of the hall flew open, crashing back on their hinges and the room was suddenly full of black clad men wearing masks and brandishing pistols. In moments they had taken up strategic positions around the room and the one who was obviously their leader was making for the platform. It was then that I noticed they all appeared to be wearing identical badges to the one Holmes had been examining the previous evening in the tower—a clenched fist and the letter "A." The Sons of Albion!

My observation was soon confirmed as the leader took up a position next to the Prince and held his pistol threateningly to the royal temple.

"Members of the world's press," he cried, "let the word go forth that the Sons of Albion have spoken this day . . ."

Despite the chaos in the room, an irreverent thought crossed my mind. I could not help but think that so populist a movement might be better advised to adopt a less biblical form of address in future. I was also struck with the distinct impression that neither McDoum nor von Bork seemed as surprised or outraged by this intrusion as they should have been but now I was fairly sure that what we were watching was of their devising. But just how far were they prepared to go? Was their royal hostage really in danger?

But before the senior Son of Albion could develop his peroration any further and while every eye in the room was fixed on the platform drama, I became aware of movement in my peripheral vision.

With none of the theatricality we had just witnessed but with equal effectiveness, more men had drifted into the hall through a series of side doors. Some of them—I saw with a surge of pleasure—wore the uniform of a renowned Scottish regiment I had fought beside at Maiwand; others looked like members of the local constabulary. All of them were carrying rifles or revolvers.

The last man to enter through the open main doors—blowing a whistle loudly, like the referee at some sporting event—was Lestrade.

The room fell completely silent. I wish I could have taken a photograph of everyone in the room frozen for a moment into a tableau or the frieze on one of those Grecian vases.

McDoum and von Bork were open mouthed. This was clearly no part of the Master Plan. The Son of Albion looked like a defeated puppet in a seaside Punch & Judy show as he slowly lowered the pistol. The Prince himself casually rubbed his temple where it had endured the pressure, as if this were an everyday occurrence. Lestrade seemed about to say something when the tableau just as suddenly dissolved . . .

The Sons of Albion had not expected opposition but, having encountered it, they were not about to capitulate without a fight. Whether they were English mercenaries or Germans— or, more likely, a combination of the two—they gave a good account of themselves. The next thing I knew was that the two sides were locked in hand to hand conflict. Neither dared to use their weapons for fear of injuring their own men. It was a bizarre spectacle indeed—rather like a game of living chess with the journalists doing their bemused best to stay out of the way of the "pieces."

The action on the floor distracted me from the platform but now, as I looked again, it was clear that McDoum and von Bork had decided to cut their losses. After a hasty whispered consultation—and unobserved by both the warring factions—McDoum made for the door to the left of the platform, while von Bork seized the Prince's arm and with surprising strength in one so slight propelled the much heavier man towards the opposite door.

I was about to leap on to the platform and intercede when I noticed that the German had a small but lethal-looking pistol pressed to the back of the Prince's neck. A moment later they vanished from sight but I was relieved to see they were closely followed by Nemo and Buchan. As he left Buchan caught my eye and raised one thumb in salutation. He seemed to be positively enjoying himself, which was more than I could say for myself.

Where the devil was Holmes?

Then I saw him beckoning me from the doorway through which McDoum had made his escape. Avoiding the flailing bodies as best

I could, I made to join him. En route I caught a glimpse of Lestrade doing a creditable job of pounding the head of one of the Sons of Albion against the lectern. The expression of malicious glee on his face suggested that it was the first time he had had the opportunity to relieve his feelings in this particular way since his days as a policeman on the beat.

A moment later the noise of the contest between the so-called Sons of Albion and Scotland's indisputable finest was behind me. Outside the room there was not a soul to be seen—not even Holmes. The main hallway was totally deserted.

I hissed his name in something of a stage whisper.

"In here, old fellow," I heard from a nearby room.

I hurried inside—only to find him standing in front of a mirror and calmly removing the elements of his disguise. In front of my eyes Quentin E. Dowd was transformed back into Sherlock Holmes.

"Don't worry, Watson," Holmes smiled back at me from the mirror image. "The great advantage of an island is its insularity. McDoum is going nowhere—and nor will he wish to until he has, as he believes, obliterated all traces of his present identity.

"Ah, that's better," he added, inspecting his handiwork. "There's something I find curiously restrictive about the North American persona. Watson, remind me not to return in some other life as a Red Indian. And now it is time for a man to meet his nemesis. Oh no, not *me,* my dear chap—I *am* the nemesis . . ."

From the confident way he led me through corridors and around corners, it was obvious that Holmes—with his usual thoroughness—had explored the terrain in advance. Most of the doors were firmly closed and Holmes soon deterred me from trying to open them.

"I fancy I know where our friend is to be found," he said, then motioned me to silence as we approached one that was standing ajar. From inside I could hear the sound of someone opening and closing drawers in a hurry.

I looked at Holmes, who nodded—a little sadly, I thought. Then, raising a hand, indicating that I should stand my ground, he slipped into the room. I edged my way closer and peered through the crack . . .

At which moment I seemed to take leave of my senses.

The room was full of people—but they were all the same person!

McDoum was standing behind an antique desk, frenziedly emptying the contents of its drawers into a large leather portmanteau but, other than that, the room was totally unfurnished and empty—except for dozens of identical images of McDoum doing precisely the same thing.

It was then I realised that I was looking at the Hall of Mirrors from my dream, the endless repetition of the things one fears most.

I must have gasped aloud for McDoum suddenly looked up. Or rather, *all* the McDoums looked up as one.

Obviously, there was no way he could see me but he did find himself staring at Holmes, who now moved into my line of vision, too. Multiple McDoums confronting Holmes after Holmes after Holmes . . .

And then Holmes did an unexpected thing. Although it was scarcely mid-afternoon, no daylight penetrated the room. A single candelabrum on the desk and the reflections from the mirrored walls illuminated the scene like the inside of one of those kaleidoscopes we all used to peer into as children. The effect here was that of two actors on a lighted stage.

Until Holmes swept the candelabrum to the floor.

Some of the flames continued to flicker weakly but the room was suddenly transformed into one of Dante's Circles of Hell. Sometimes the images of the two men were fairly clear, then they would jump and tower over each other. It was impossible to see where one ended and the other began and I could see that Holmes was now moving around the room, changing his position in relation to the stationary McDoum, who seemed transfixed to the spot.

Finally he spoke. His voice was harsh and scarcely above a whisper.

"What the devil are you doing here, Geier? I have no time to . . ."

And then I swear that, if I ever heard the sound of fear, it was in that man's tone.

"*Holmes?* But you can't be? You're . . ."

"Dead?" Holmes's voice seemed to echo eerily around the room, as if he were a ventriloquist throwing his voice from image to image. Was this perhaps one more of the many skills that he had not yet chosen to reveal?

"I'm sorry to disappoint your expectations, McDoum . . . Or will you now be reverting to—Moriarty?"

Holmes spoke the name casually but the effect could not have been more dramatic on the two listeners.

I felt my own heart thump in my chest. Moriarty? Holmes's old arch enemy, the man he dubbed "the Napoleon of Crime," the man he had grappled with that fateful day on the rocks over the Reichenbach Falls. But surely Moriarty had finally died last year when, wounded by my own bullet, he had allowed himself to drop into the swirling Thames from the House of Commons parapet and we had subsequently viewed his damaged corpse. Or—as Holmes had insisted—*a* corpse. Had we been dealing with his reincarnation? And why had Holmes kept it to himself?

But if the effect on me was akin to walking into an invisible wall, that one word produced a frightening reaction from the man behind the desk.

I heard a low hiss, as though someone had opened a basket and released a nest of vipers.

Then I heard—"You meddling fool. This is not some footling matter for your armchair games. You are dealing with forces far beyond your puny powers—forces that will tread you under foot without even noticing."

"Possibly, possibly. Though I am inclined to wonder why you and your so-called 'friends' have expended so much of that force on such an elaborate game with me. A little less attention to Holmes and a little more to Siegfried and—who knows . . . ?"

"So you know about Siegfried? Ah well, it is of little matter in the scheme of things. Behind Siegfried are others I will not bore you with. Suffice it to say, they are as many and as relentless as the waves that will continue to pound these island shores until they wash it quite away."

One had to allow a sneaking respect for the man's ability to recover a degree of composure so quickly. And then from my vantage point

I noticed something that Holmes was almost certainly unable to see.

McDoum's hand was stealthily moving toward his jacket pocket and it did not take much imagination to deduce what might be in it. He was merely talking to hold Holmes's attention and distract him.

What was I to do? I drew my own trusty service revolver and prayed that some guidance would be given to me.

In the event the circumstances dictated what happened next.

Before I even saw it McDoum had produced a pistol and fired at the wall opposite him. Without even taking time to think, I pushed open the door and rushed into the room.

One of the mirrors was shattered and lying in fragments on the ground but in all the rest I could see the shifting image of Holmes, which appeared to be engaged in some macabre dance around the room.

McDoum fired again and another image disintegrated before my eyes.

Now I could see that there was a secondary figure in each of them—the man behind the desk. When McDoum was shooting at his opponent, by this ironic visual distortion he was also firing at himself!

A third shot and a third Holmes and McDoum imploded.

"Come, Moriarty," I heard Holmes's taunting voice say. "Six shots for a shilling. No fairground owner need worry about you!"

His words enraged his enemy, as no doubt Holmes had calculated they would. McDoum loosed off more shots and for a moment the room was full of flying fragments of glass. When the reverberations died away, the effect was like looking into a mouth full of missing teeth. Even so, McDoum had failed to deplete the ghostly gallery to any marked extent. Holmes's image still shimmered around the room.

And then McDoum became aware that they were no longer alone. I must have moved my position and caught his eye in one of the reflections, for he swung round and pointed his pistol at me. Since mine was already pointing at him, we were now both, so to speak, "in check."

I knew I could take no further chances and pulled the trigger.

As I did so, I was subliminally aware of two things simultaneously. The first was of Holmes saying—from far away at the bottom of some tunnel—"Unless I miss my guess, that is a Browning and fires six bullets. By my reckoning, Moriarty, your turn is over. Unless, of course, you wish to venture another shilling?"

The second, thank Heaven—was the empty click of McDoum's useless pistol.

A moment later the man was looking at me with

an air of slight surprise, as though I were a guest whose name he couldn't quite recall. Then he looked down at his shirt, where a red carnation of blood was slowly blossoming.

And then his body was on the floor at my feet.

Except in the heat of battle, I have rarely fired at another human being in anger. My life, in fact, has been dedicated to saving life. The realisation of what I had just done made me feel temporarily faint.

I was aware of Holmes by my side and both of us looking down at what had been McDoum or Moriarty. From far away I heard Holmes saying—

"The mirror crack'd from side to side
'The curse is come upon me,' cried
The Lady of Shalott.

Do you know, Watson, I sometimes feel that Tennyson has almost as many appropriate words to offer as our friend, the Bard."

"Holmes, what . . . ?" was all I could think of to say.

"Oh, our little trick with smoke and mirrors? Not nearly as risky as it might appear, old fellow. When one considers the mathematical options of those multiple reflections, the dim light and then factors in the psychological tension at work on a man who is facing a ghost, I believe I was giving myself reasonable odds. Nonetheless, I must admit it was modestly reassuring to know that Messrs. Watson and Eley were—shall we say?—waiting in the wings."

We knelt down and turned the body over. By the light spilling in from the door I had thrown open when I entered, the face looked strangely at peace.

"So this is finally the end of Moriarty?" I said, as much to myself as to Holmes.

"Of *a* Moriarty—but, alas, not of *the* Moriarty. The recently deceased is, admittedly, one Colonel James Moriarty. But then, Mrs. Moriarty—for some reason best known to herself—gave two of her three sons the identical Christian name. Her third son, whose name temporarily escapes me, was, to the best of my knowledge, a railway guard. As you see, confusion at best and duplicity at worst would appear to run in the Moriarty psyche."

Then, dropping the apparent levity like a discarded coat, he continued . . .

"I have known for some time that James Moriarty the elder . . ."—and he indicated the man at our feet—"was intermittently—and at first, I sense, reluctantly—involved in his brother's evil empire. Then, it seems, blood started to tell and I began to receive information of a new pattern of behaviour emerging that was all too familiar. Finally, about two years ago, he vanished entirely from the scene—at almost precisely the moment when a transformation seemed to come over the previously retiring Sir Angus McDoum."

"So Moriarty became McDoum?"

"So it would appear. Clearly, as it now appears, at the behest of his brother . . ."

"But what happened to the real McDoum?"

"That we shall discover in due course but, I confess, Watson, I am not optimistic. Human life does not count for a great deal with these people. And in their terms there was, indeed, a great deal at stake. No less than the future of our country— and perhaps several others besides."

"But what did Moriarty hope to gain—the *real* Moriarty, I mean?"

"Power, old fellow—power. The ultimate aphrodisiac. Knowing Moriarty's mentality, he would act as the agent for German imperialism in exchange for their allowing him these islands of ours as his effective fiefdom. Not that he would be overtly head of state . . ." he added, anticipating my objection—"No, some convenient charismatic puppet would be used for that purpose. But never doubt that the hand pulling the puppet's strings would be Moriarty's."

"But what happens now?"

"Now there will be one more entry in his ledger—heavily underscored—to my debit. And when this sorry episode is over—which, I fancy, it soon will be—why, he will fade into the background until a more propitious moment. No, we have not heard the last of Professor Moriarty—although I do believe his sibling namesake has little more to say to us . . ."

His next remark jerked me unceremoniously back to the present.

"But come, Watson, I fancy Nemo and Buchan—not to mention my dear brother—may require our presence . . ."

And with that he was out of the room and making his way along the corridor, calling over his shoulder—"Don't worry about tidying up—Lestrade will take care of that when he has finished playing his games."

CHAPTER SEVENTEEN

I confess it was as much as I could do to keep up with him as he moved rapidly from one corridor and passage way to the next. Moments later we passed through a heavy door and found ourselves outside the castle and on a steep cliff path. Unlike the previous evening, the night sky was clear and the stars shone like cut diamonds on a jeweller's tray. After all these years I can still barely recognise any but the most obvious of the constellations. The one that caught my eye was that of Orion the hunter with his sword in his belt and it seemed a particularly appropriate image considering the matter in hand. As I followed Holmes along that treacherous path I fingered my service revolver and was consoled to think that there were five persuasive arguments left to us.

A few steps later we had turned a corner. Although you could still feel its presence, the castle was now behind us and the path was moving steadily downwards. Ahead I could see a small peninsula that resembled an exclamation mark jutting out from the main body of the island. By one of those freaks of nature, an arch of rock had been left linking the two. Someone—I later learned it was the monks who had inhabited an earlier structure on the site that now held the castle—had carved a primitive stone staircase into the rock to assist any unwise traveller who felt inclined to make the journey to that forlorn spit of land that jutted out into the inhospitable sea.

So these were the sixty-four steps that had caused the Germans so much discomfiture? One did not need to be a Sherlock Holmes to see that they had seen the passage of many feet over the centuries and, indeed, there was ample evidence of recent passing.

A few paces along the causeway—with a sheer drop on either side and only a slender handrail between us and oblivion—Holmes stooped and picked up a piece of material loosely tied around one of the stanchions. A glance told me at once that it was Nemo's handkerchief.

"For a man who does not exist Monsieur Nemo certainly makes his presence known," Holmes said in a tone of voice that told me he was now positively enjoying the game that was afoot.

The precipitous path took us round a corner of the headland and now we found ourselves looking at the mouth of an enormous cavern that Mother Nature and the centuries had hollowed out of the living rock. We could see lights flickering from the interior and hear muffled echoes but precisely what was going on remained for the moment a mystery.

To our left the sea was running high but not impossibly so and now that we had safely navigated the sixty-four steps—which I had, indeed, counted—I was able to risk a look around me.

It was then that I noticed a subdued light bobbing up and down some little way offshore. It was clearly the navigation light of a small vessel at anchor there. Holmes anticipated my remark.

"Operation Siegfried, Watson. The hero's triumphal barge—or not, as the case may be."

With that we had reached the entrance of the cavern and he pulled urgently at my sleeve to enjoin me to silence. At his nod I was the first to edge my way round the last rock and as I took in the amazing scene that confronted me . . .

"Ah, good evening again, Major—or should I say, Doctor? Oh, please do not think that you deceived us for one moment with your pathetic disguise. It was always in our calculations that you would seek to avenge your late and—by me—quite unlamented friend. I wonder what the great Sherlock Holmes would say, were he able to be here now?"

"I should probably quote the Scots poet, Robbie Burns to the effect that 'the best laid plans of mice and men gang aft agley'—but then, that might tax even *your* excellent English, von Bork. I believe Mr. Burns' inflections give trouble even to—shall we say?—certain sons of Albion . . .

Do pardon my late arrival but I had to check my appearance in the mirror before I felt able to join your little party."

And Holmes made an entrance that even Irving would have envied.

I wish I could adequately describe the tableau in that Stygian cavern with the sea lapping at our feet. Where Holmes and I stood was in reality an extension of the cliff path. Two or three feet above us—giving all the appearance of a stage—was a natural plateau that man's efforts had undoubtedly improved upon. On it stood the Prince with Zuberbier's pistol clapped to his head and what appeared to be an expression of wry resignation on his face. Behind and to one side of him a group of uniformed German sailors were dourly guarding their British equivalents, who were herded together with their hands on their heads. Beyond the plateau the cave faded away into impenetrable darkness and I could not even guess at its true dimensions.

It was then that I remembered the whole *raison d'être* for this place, so concerned had I been with Moriarty and the events at the castle. Of course— *The Phantom*! My country's secret weapon and perhaps our last best hope in what was all too obviously the precise scenario Mycroft had laid before me that day at the Diogenes Club. We had played our hand—and we had lost!

For there in the gloom in the furthest recesses

of what I now regarded as the tomb of our hopes I could make out the outlines of the submarine.

It was both huge and sleek—a killer whale that would have confounded any modern day Ahab. In my mind's eye I could see it ruthlessly hunting down our enemies and consigning them to the deep. But now . . .

Holmes moved ahead of me and, as he did so, I could have sworn he murmured—"Remember Alice in the Looking Glass, old friend. Remember Alice . . ."

His movement broke the spell. Von Bork was the first to unfreeze and I have to admit the fellow regained his composure with remarkable speed. One moment his jaw was agape with disbelief, the next he was once more the arrogant Prussian *junker*. In the split second between the two states, though, his eyes revealed every last thought that was passing through that astute brain of his.

How can Holmes be alive? What has happened to Moriarty? The most transient of thoughts, that the man was expendable. What *else* had he miscalculated and how might it affect the greater scheme of things? And then finally the tiniest of lopsided smiles. For, after all, who was pointing the weapons at whom?

Now he raised his own pistol—a German Luger, I noticed and motioned us to join the group. Holmes obeyed—with apparent reluctance—and I noticed he seemed, by accident or design, to use his body to block the view of the sea from those standing in the cave. Or was I imagining it?

" 'Check,' I believe," he said, looking up at von Bork.

"Do you really think so, Holmes?" the other replied. "I'm afraid I don't see it that way at all. Certainly you have disturbed the even tenor of our original plan. It would have been so much simpler if our 'Sons of Albion' could simply have threatened to abduct his Royal Highness here, only to have their machinations foiled by these good old German boys, who just happened to be paying a friendly visit from their conveniently nearby ship. The world's press on hand to report it. A grateful nation . . . a groundswell of emotional thanks to our good neighbours . . . you can write the rest for yourself."

"I imagine much of it is *already* written and ready to be set into type?" Holmes replied laconically.

"Well, yes, and I hate to see waste in any form but—what is your English phrase?—'one cannot make an omelette without breaking the egg'? No, I'm afraid that we must adjust our tactics to meet the changed circumstances. Now, what would Clausewitz recommend on this occasion, I wonder? Such a poet and philosopher on the art of warfare, dear Carl . . ."

His index finger played around his upper lip in much the same gesture that I have seen Holmes use and I wondered whether this was his way of parodying the man he finally had at his mercy. There was no doubt about it—von Bork was playing cat and mouse with us.

"Ah, I have it, gentlemen. A less elegant solution, I fear, than I had first intended but then, the situation in which we now find ourselves is largely of your making, I would suggest.

"I'm afraid there will be an unfortunate accident here in which the heir to the British throne, while visiting a top secret naval installation, is not only abducted by terrorists but is also the victim of an explosion, which, incidentally, totally destroys a vessel which had been critical to the nation's interests. A party of German sailors happen to be in the vicinity. Hearing the explosion, they arrive on the scene but, alas, they are too late to save the unfortunate victims. Later there will be speculation that there was foul play involved as two of the corpses will be identified as those of the now notorious Sherlock Holmes—whom the police had recently suspected of a series of brutal murders—and his acolyte, Doctor Watson. Yes, I think that will serve quite well."

I looked wildly at my friend, only to find him languidly examining his finger nails. He might have been a tutor listening to a promising pupil read his dissertation. Finally he looked up.

"Interesting, very interesting. Yet I believe it

leaves out a few of the salient facts. How does it strike you, your Royal Highness?"

Again I was reminded of the way the characters on a stage exchange prepared dialogue. All eyes were now turned on the Prince.

"I am inclined to agree, Mr. Holmes. If I remember my Clausewitz, did he not say something to the effect that the first rule of battle was to know thine enemy? In that respect, my dear von Bork, you fail signally. C minus."

And with that the future monarch carefully began to peel off his moustache and beard, wincing as he did so.

"My dear Sherlock, you really must give me some tutoring in the application of spirit gum and facial hair. I fear I have used too much, for it is damnably painful," said Mycroft Holmes.

And then I saw that once again I had seen but not observed—if you see what I mean?

There were few men that Mycroft could possibly have impersonated because of his vast bulk but—as luck would have it—Prince Edward was one of them. I had been staring at him in that castle hall and seeing what I *expected* to see—as had everyone else.

Now the pieces began to fall into place. Mycroft's mission to dissuade the Prince had not been in vain after all. And although we were still "in check," as Holmes put it, thank heaven the Royal Family were safe!

And then the world began to spin out of control . . .

Surprised as they undoubtedly were by this turn of events, von Bork and his men had somehow managed to keep their weapons trained on us all. They were distracted but by no means disarmed. But all this was to change in an instant.

For suddenly two new figures marched out of the gloom that enshrouded the recesses of the cave. Their faces impassive, they marched with military precision until they reached the edge of the human circle, then snapped to attention. The total surprise created by their appearance—no less than by their demeanour—caused the whole group to freeze and not one of the German guards made the slightest effort to stop them.

I could hardly believe my eyes. The two men were Buchan and Nemo.

The unexpected became the surrealistic as the two men then began to sing . . .

Allons, enfants de la patrie,
Le jour de gloire est arrivé . . .

To be honest, their performance would not have stood the scrutiny of the Gallery at the Old Mo' but in its present context it more than served its purpose. Their voices echoed and re-echoed around this natural echo chamber—Nemo's passionately Gallic almost drowning out

Buchan's highland drone. Their audience stood rooted to the spot in total silence, as if we were listening to the de Reskes at Covent Garden.

Qu'un sang impur
Abreuve nos sillons!

As the last notes died away, there was a moment of complete silence and then the bizarre sound of two pairs of hands clapping. Holmes and Mycroft were actually applauding!

Never mind the Looking Glass—this was Alice in Wonderland all over again. *Nothing* was as it seemed.

What could possibly happen next?

That question was soon answered as the "stage" was suddenly filled with "extras." From the far reaches of the cave from which Nemo and Buchan had emerged came a virtual "chorus" of British sailors, rifles at the ready, far out-numbering their German counterparts, who sensibly and rapidly threw down their own weapons. No false heroics here. It would be hard to imagine a more dramatic *volte face*.

Holmes stepped over to von Bork and delicately removed the Luger from frozen fingers. As he did so, I saw the purpose of his rather awkward manner of entering the cave. Standing in the narrow aperture were more of our men and a small boat bobbing gently nearby, effectively blocking any escape by sea, told the story of how they came to be there.

"Checkmate," said Holmes in a voice devoid of any emotion, least of all satisfaction, "unless, of course, you have another move in mind?"

Perhaps it was the unfortunate choice of words that precipitated what happened next.

Von Bork shook himself like a man coming out of a deep sleep, then looked wildly around him. Before any of us could anticipate his action, he had picked something up from a pile near his feet and seemed to throw it at Mycroft, who instinctively ducked.

But now it became clear that he had a quite different intention, for he screamed something unintelligible in German and I saw that the object was intended for Zuberbier, who had remained standing next to the "Prince" during the recent confusion.

Everything now seemed to happen in slow motion.

I found my eyes rivetted on the object von Bork had thrown. It looked just like an ordinary domestic candle and then the penny dropped. A stick of dynamite!

Slowly—oh, so slowly—Zuberbier stretched out a hand and made a catch that would have been commendable in a slip fielder at Lord's.

The next moment things went back to normal— or as normal as these abnormal circumstances could permit. Now both sides were in a state of shock and could only stand helplessly by as the German turned and raced for the far side of the cavern, where *The Phantom* rode at anchor. A moment later he had leapt down the other, steeper side of the plateau and was lost to view.

"My God, Holmes," I cried, "we must stop him."

But Holmes grabbed my arm with surprising force and prevented me from giving pursuit. I could see that Nemo was using the same restraint on Buchan.

"No, old friend, things must take their course."

The silence that followed was broken only by the sound of Zuberbier's running footsteps distorted by the acoustics of the cavern. And then they stopped and slowly the echoes died away. We were like the cast of a play rivetted by the unseen actions of an off-stage character.

Then came the most almighty explosion. It threw all of us, friend and foe alike, to the floor of the cave and the reverberations bounced off the curved walls, assaulting us almost physically. The only consolation was that I could both feel and hear the pain, for my medical knowledge told me instinctively that a blast of this magnitude—concentrated by its location—could easily result in permanent deafness.

Fragments began to rain down on us and it was some time before, one by one, we began to get to our feet and brush ourselves down.

"Holmes, Mycroft—are you all right?" I cried and was greatly relieved to hear their positive responses. "It's an absolute miracle we survived."

"Fortuitous, perhaps," Holmes replied, picking up one of the larger fragments from the floor near his feet, "but miraculous? I think not."

By now two British sailors had pulled von Bork unceremoniously to his feet and the other Germans were being herded into a group, their previous confidence of manner now quite dissipated. Instead they looked cowed and defeated—with the sole exception of von Bork himself.

His eyes had their old glitter as he pulled himself erect and turned to face Holmes. The suicidal death of his henchman clearly bothered him not at all.

"So, my friend, we have at least the satisfaction of knowing that your precious *Phantom* is now—a phantom, *ja*?" And he threw back his head in a full-hearted laugh, which stopped when he realised that he was not achieving the expected shocked reaction. Holmes, Mycroft and Nemo—who had now joined the group—were, in fact, looking mildly amused at the German's performance. I exchanged questioning glances with Buchan, who was obviously just as much in the dark as I was.

"*Nein*, I'm afraid, von Bork," Holmes replied, carefully weighing the object in his hand and not bothering to even look at his opponent. "You see, a phantom is, by definition, an illusion, a deception, a figment of the imagination. As such you could hardly expect to find it where you expected it to be, my dear fellow, now could you? What you saw was an *ersatz* phantom. Here—the least we can do for you is to give you a small souvenir of your holiday in the highlands . . ."

And he handed von Bork the object he had been holding. It was painted a dull black on one side and looked like metal but by the way von Bork misjudged its weight, it was obviously significantly lighter than it appeared.

"Balsa wood, von Bork. A balsa wood replica *Phantom*. The real *Phantom* left here several nights ago when your ship was sighted heading in this direction—on the principle of one being company but two a distinct crowd. But don't worry—you will undoubtedly meet her on some more propitious occasion."

Von Bork looked thoughtfully at the useless fragment he was holding, then casually tossed it into the water. When he looked up I was amazed to see that he seemed to have recovered his composure completely. The piercing eyes found those of Holmes and it was as if two medieval knights were assessing each other's strength before the next round of battle. Will clashed with will.

"One of the more difficult concepts I have had to try and understand while living on your

barbaric island is that of being a 'good loser.'
To me it seems a contradiction in terms. I must
concede that you have won this round, Mr.
Sherlock Holmes, but it is *only* a round and there
will be others. And those you shall *not* win. Taste
the fruits of victory while you can, my friend,
before they turn sour in your mouth." Then,
indicating his bedraggled band of followers—
"So what happens now?"

"If I had my way," I cried before I could stop
myself, "I'd shoot the lot of you!"

Before I could say any more Mycroft loomed
over us.

"The Doctor's sentiments, while a little
immoderate in their expression, would almost
certainly be shared by many of our fellow
citizens. You have, after all, willfully interfered
in the affairs of a country at peace with and
officially friendly to your own. Were the events
of recent weeks to become public knowledge, the
international repercussions would undoubtedly
be most serious. Which is why they will remain
unknown . . ."

Seeing that I was about to burst out again, he
put a calming hand on my arm.

"Yes, Doctor, that is the decision of Her
Majesty's Government. Were he here, I know
the Prime Minister would like to thank you and
your fellow conspirators, von Bork, for making
apparent what he has long suspected. I can assure

you that there will be far less foot dragging in the corridors of Westminster in the months and years ahead, thanks to the signal service you have rendered us this day."

Von Bork's eyes now shone like chips of ice and the muscles in his jaw seemed about to snap. The one thing his Prussian soul could not abide was ridicule of any kind—something Mycroft understood instinctively.

"I repeat my question," said the German. "What happens now?"

"Oh, a number of things, my dear fellow." It was Holmes's turn to twist the knife.

"In my country,"—this was Nemo—"we should say—'*rassemblez les suspects habituels*' or 'round up the usual suspects'. . . ."

"I think you can safely assume that the process is already under way," boomed Mycroft. "Even as we speak there are certain 'fellow travellers' who will unaccountably fail to reach their destinations. Graf von Bork, alas, cannot be one of them on this occasion. He is a guest of Her Majesty by virtue of his diplomatic passport and must be returned to sender in mint condition . . ."

"Although I suspect there may be occasions in the weeks ahead when he will have cause to wish that he had extended his stay with us," Holmes smiled humourlessly. "The hero is hardly likely to be hailed as conquering in his own land. Quite the reverse, I fear. And now, von Bork, like Cleopatra, your barge awaits. I believe one of your own vessels is moored conveniently, if a trifle anxiously, a little way offshore? Please convey our best regards to the Kaiser and thank you for opening our eyes."

He gestured towards the opening of the cavern. I could now see that a series of dinghies had arrived, each of them manned by impassive armed sailors. On a sign from Mycroft their colleagues on the plateau began herding the Germans toward them like so many sheep.

Only von Bork stood his ground for the moment. You had to grant the devil his due, he certainly was a cool customer. His eyes moved from one of us to the next—Holmes, Mycroft, Nemo, Buchan, myself—as if to imprint every detail of our features in his memory. I have to confess I felt a small chill in the middle of my spine, which was ridiculous, considering that we had won hands down.

When he finally spoke, however, he seemed to be looking at no one in particular but at somewhere beyond us in the far distance.

"This sorry little episode has confirmed one thing for me, gentlemen. There is a rift between our two races that is much wider than this pathetic drop of water. It is one of attitude. We Germans are professionals. You British like to call yourselves 'gifted amateurs.' This time the professionals took you too lightly but next time it will be very different and in the end the dedicated professional will always defeat the inspired amateur."

"At least we believe in inspiration not obsession," I cried. But if von Bork heard me, he gave no sign.

Snapping off an ironic military salute, he turned smartly on his heel and made for the nearest boat. I seemed to catch a faint *"Auf widersehen."* A few moments later the entrance to the cavern was empty.

"Well, Holmes?" I turned to him, expecting to see that lean face looking stony-eyed after the departed enemy. Instead the eyes were sparkling, as if his veins were charged with at the very least a seven per cent solution. The man was positively *enjoying* himself!

Almost to himself he murmured—"I shall certainly see *you* again. But whether you will see *me* . . ."

Then, reading my expression, he smiled—a trifle guiltily, I thought—and turned to Mycroft.

"Now then, brother mine, an appropriate quotation for the occasion? *Not* Tennyson, I think. *Or* the Bard . . ."

As they left the stage, so to speak, and Mycroft began to heave himself laboriously up the stone staircase, I heard him humouring his brother with . . .

"Spenser?

That darksome cave they enter, where
  they find
That cursed man, low sitting on the ground."

Then, as they moved further away from us, I
heard Holmes answer—
  "Or what about Coleridge?

  Through wood and dale the sacred river ran,
  Then reach'd the caverns measureless to
    man,
  And sank in tumult to a lifeless ocean:
  And 'mid this tumult Kubla heard from far
  Ancestral voices prophesying war!

A perceptive fellow, Coleridge, I fear . . ."
  And then their voices faded on the night air . . .
  I became aware of someone plucking at my
sleeve and turned to find young Buchan whose
eyes were hardly less bright than Holmes's had
been a moment earlier.
  "Why that was a bonnie affair, Doctor," he said,
for all the world as though I had arranged it for
his personal amusement. "But I was thinking—
there's a grand wee story in it somewhere, isn't
there now? Oh, not the *real* story"—he added
hastily—"but a made up one, like.
  "I was thinking," he added pensively, "of
something like *The Sixty-Four Steps*. You're a
literary man, Doctor. How does that strike you?

Or—no—that doesn't sound quite right. What about *The Thirty-Nine Steps*? More of a flow to it?"

For the first time in days I felt on strong ground. Putting a fatherly arm on his shoulder—which also proved helpful in ascending those damned stairs—I said, as kindly as I knew how . . .

"Buchan, my boy. I think you'll find a title like that will never fly. The reading public want something more—catchy. When I come to write my own account, I shall probably go for something like *The Case of the Double Detective*. You see what I mean? Catchy."

It's one of the few consolations of advancing years that one can set these young fellows straight from time to time.

CHAPTER EIGHTEEN

I confess our rooms in 221B had never seemed cosier or more welcoming than they did that evening a few days later, when we were sitting by the fire with the curtains shutting out one of London's typically early winter evenings. I fancy we had both had enough of that Scottish mist to last us for some time to come.

We had arrived back at the castle to find a flushed but triumphant Lestrade lecturing the so-called "Sons of Albion" like the proverbial Dutch uncle. Ought to be ashamed of themselves . . . taking the German shilling—or mark or whatever the deuce it calls itself . . . he had the particulars of every man jack of them, that he did, and they could be sure that Scotland Yard would have its eye on them from here to Kingdom Come. If it hadn't been for the Powers-That-Be deciding to say no more about it for the country's greater good, well . . . and much more in that vein.

A fishing boat of sorts had been found and the last we saw of what turned out to be a very mixed bag of mercenaries was a set of green faces leaning over the side as it pitched and yawed its way back to the mainland.

Lestrade had made one further discovery in our absence. While searching the castle for possible stragglers, he and his men had heard suspicious sounds from one of the cellars. Having broken down the door, they discovered the real Sir Angus McDoum and two of his senior retainers. They had been held under the equivalent of house arrest by Moriarty and von Bork, being incarcerated in the cellars when visitors to the island were expected. For a reputedly taciturn man, Sir Angus had much to say on the subject of Anglo-German relations and I was left with the clear conviction that the House of Commons would sit up and take notice of him in future. Even as Holmes and I took our leave, Lestrade was making copious notes in one of those dog-eared notebooks that were his constant companions.

Back on the mainland I stood a pace or two back as the two brothers said their own farewells.

"Well, Sherlock?"

"Well, Your Royal Highness?"

"I must confess I quite enjoyed the way people bowed and scraped to me. It could become addictive. Oh, and by the way, a certain Lady is likely to wish to express her appreciation once again. I don't suppose . . . ?"

"I'm afraid not."

"But there has to be *something* . . . An emerald tie-pin last time, I believe?"

"Yes. Cuff links to match, perhaps?"

"*Fait accompli.*"

And then for the one and only time in my life I saw those two unlikely brothers embrace.

The evening paper landed at my feet in an ill-folded heap.

As I picked it up and began to return it to some semblance of order, Holmes leaned back in his chair, put his hands behind his head and stretched those long legs to the fire.

"I am encouraged, Watson, to see that I have fortunately survived the 'Yorkshire Moors Horror.'" And with one foot he indicated the relevant page of the newspaper. Scooping it up, I read the account the Yard had placed purporting to explain the confusion over Holmes's reported death. True to form the paper's editorial was effusive in its relief that "this remarkable man" would once again be able to "purge the Evil from our callous society."

I was on the point of saying that "this remarkable man" had better be careful not to believe all he read about himself in the press, when my eye was caught by another story, this time on the front page.

I found myself reading it aloud . . .

GERMANS SEE A GHOST: CHAOS AT NAVAL SHOW!

There was consternation—followed by official apologies from the Admiralty—when the annual German *Seefest* off the coast of Bremen was interrupted today by the unexpected surfacing of *H.M.S. Phantom*, Britain's revolutionary new submarine.

Observers from the world's major naval powers witnessed a bizarre spectacle as the prototype top secret vessel dramatically interrupted the manoeuvres of the crack German fleet.

"It was as though the sub was playing games with the other ships," an American observer commented later, "it ran rings around them. I'll bet Kaiser Bill had a red face that night!"

The *Seefest* is generally considered a show piece for German naval achievement. Official sources were naturally reticent . . .

"By Jove, Holmes, that's clipped their wings and no mistake!"

I lowered the paper to find him staring deeply into the fire.

"Yes, old fellow, it has indeed. But a bird's wings don't stay clipped forever. I fear the German eagle will fly again and next time its temper may not be so controlled. It may turn and rend. And let us not forget that 'Kaiser Bill' still has the Napoleon of Crime to aid him.

"We have bought ourselves time and very little

more. No, the clouds are gathering and, as we stood on that benighted isle I could swear I felt a cold wind coming from the north, Watson. Let us hope our fellow countrymen feel it, too, for it will leave a killing frost wherever it touches. My hope—my prayer even—is that von Bork and his kind are too arrogant to learn the lesson of these past few weeks. He was once heard to say that a more docile, simple folk could not be imagined. We must hope he *still* thinks so, for in that lies our best defence. It is for us to know and for the German jackals to find out that we British are a hardy breed, perversely never more so than when our feet are numb and our hands are chill . . ."

Then he looked up and his mood changed, as if by an effort of will.

"But that is then and this is now. Both my hands and feet are comfortably warm—so much so that, if I do not bestir myself, I shall find myself dozing like an old man in the chimney corner. Now then, my dear fellow, if you can stir *yourself* sufficiently to make some sense of that newspaper you have so selfishly abused, I believe I noticed a Verdi programme at the Albert Hall this evening.

"A little overblown lyricism might not go amiss for once, don't you think? For some reason I am not in the mood for Wagner."

Center Point Large Print
600 Brooks Road / PO Box 1
Thorndike, ME 04986-0001 USA

(207) 568-3717

US & Canada:
1 800 929-9108
www.centerpointlargeprint.com